SPEAK

A POST DIVORCE ROMANCE

J.L. SEEGARS

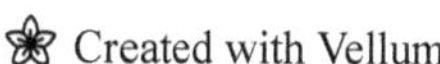 Created with Vellum

For everyone still holding on to things that no longer serve them. It's okay to let go.

Sometimes letting things go is an act of far greater power than defending or hanging on.

— ECKHART TOLLE

AUTHOR NOTE

Please be aware this story involves sensitive topics such emotional and psychological abuse as well as a brief mention of financial abuse. I encourage you to consider your own health and well-being before diving into Grayson and Xavier's story.

THE PLAYLIST

01./ You Don't Do It For Me Anymore by Demi Lovato
02./ Happier Than Ever by ASTN
03./ Lose You to Love Me by Selena Gomez
04./ Treasure in the Hills by Leon Thomas
05./ DJ Play a Love Song (ft. Twista) by Jamie Foxx
06./ Sex With Me by Rihanna
07./ luther by Kendrick Lamar & SZA
08./ Sad Corny F**k by JP Saxe
09./ You & I by Avant
10./ Halo by Beyoncé
11./ Easy by ASTN
12./ Speak by Jhené Aiko

Listen on Apple Music

1

GRAYSON

"You never look at me like that."

The damning realization, which I had planned to keep locked inside my mind, hangs in the cavern of space between Brian and I, seeping into the lush leather of the bench seat in the back of the blacked out town car he insisted we take to his firm's annual Christmas party. He claimed we needed a driver because he knew the drinks would be free flowing and he wanted to partake without worrying about how we were going to get home, but now, as I take in the vast amount of space between my body and his, I can't help but feel like distance was the point.

Like he wanted me near, but not close.

That's been the theme of the night. Us in the same room but never talking, never touching, barely speaking. Me, on the margins of conversation and at the back of his mind while all of his attention and affection went to her.

Noelle Caspen.

Just the thought of her name sends old hurts and insecurities shimmering down my spine, awaking memories of being a love sick teenager watching the boy she loved publicly give another girl things he only ever deigned to gift her in private. I've worked hard to let go of those days, to forgive Brian for being the type of shallow kid who was ashamed of liking the bigger girl, to heal the part of myself that was so desperate for love she accepted scraps of it.

On any given day, I'd confidently say that I've moved past all of that, but today it couldn't feel further from the truth. And how could it when I've just been subjected to hours of watching my husband of six years look at his high school sweetheart like she hung the fucking moon while acting like I don't exist at all? How could it when there's so much distance between us and the car is quiet, but he still doesn't hear me when I speak?

All at once, anger swells inside of me, and I no longer want to keep the realization to myself. I want it out in the open. I want acknowledgment and answers and a fucking apology.

"Brian."

His head snaps up, and eyes that are a cross between gray and green find my face for what feels like the first time since we left our home earlier this evening. Annoyance flickers in his irises as they bounce between me and the phone in his hand.

"What is it, Grayson?"

"Did you hear what I said?"

"No."

Once again, his attention shifts, returning to the open text thread on his lit screen. Noelle's name is at the top of it. Feeling bolder than usual, I slide across the seat and take the phone from him, locking it before I toss it over my shoulder.

Brian's jaw clenches, outrage rippling underneath clean shaven chestnut skin. "If you wanted my attention, all you had to do was ask for it. There's no need to resort to childish antics."

The reprimand lands where they always do: right in the center of my chest, stealing the bit of confidence I just had. I feel it leave me in a slow, painful leak that's quieted by the sound of an apology where there should be an argument. Where there should be words that tell him I shouldn't have to ask for his attention when he just demonstrated how freely he can give it to her.

"I'm sorry," I murmur, tears gathering in my eyes because I'm embarrassed at having gone to such great lengths to get him to tune into a conversation about my insecurities and his perceived slights. Because that's all it was, right? My warped perception and insecurities layered on top of a moment between old friends who haven't seen each other in years.

He nods and holds out his hand. "Thank you. Now give me back my phone."

Reaching behind me, I grab the phone at the exact moment another message comes through. I don't mean to look, but my eyes still snag on the name and the previewed content of the message on the screen. There are several messages, the last of which is just THANK YOU. THANK YOU. THANK YOU!!!! in all caps. My fingers hover over the screen, prepared to unlock the phone and figure out exactly what Noelle is thanking him for, but Brian is too quick. He pulls the phone out of my grasp and pockets it, throwing me a withering gaze from between furrowed brows.

"Were you seriously going to read my messages? That's a huge invasion of privacy," he scoffs.

"What is she thanking you for?" I ask, ignoring the statement that smacks of hypocrisy.

"What?"

"Noelle. In her last message to you, she said thank you. What did you do for her?"

Brian sighs hard and brushes lint that's not there off of his pants. "Her business is in danger of going under. I offered to help her out."

As a lawyer, Brian has always prided himself on being a strategic communicator, saying what needs to be said and only that. Giving as little information as possible while making the person he's speaking to feel like they've gotten every morsel necessary to fuel their understanding. Most of the time, it takes me hours, or sometimes even days, to untangle the web of his phrasing and garner true meaning, but tonight, understanding dawns on me with startling clarity.

While we were waiting in line for drinks—Brian and Noelle in front of me with his hand at the small of her back and my heart in my throat—Noelle droned on and on about the troubled clothing line she's been trying to launch for three years now. Brian hung on her every word, all sympathy and understanding while she talked about the difficulties of finding designers who wouldn't take issue with her stamping her name and face on their hard work.

That was the image in my mind a few minutes ago when it occurred to me that he never looks at me the way he looks at Noelle. When I realized that in all the years of us knowing each other he never once listened as intently to me when I wanted to share the wins or losses as it related to Elysian—the plus size clothing brand I started in college and gave up at the height of its success because he said the stress of running a business was stopping me from getting pregnant. When it dawned on me that among the long list of things Brian has offered me regarding my business and dreams—criticism, discouragement, flat out refusal to support me when I said just last month that I wanted to quit my job as a personal assistant to chef and restauranter, Jaxon Daniels, to revive the brand help has never been one of them.

"How?"

"For the love of God, Grayson," he groans. "Please speak in complete sentences."

"How did you help her, Brian?" I grit out. "What assistance did you provide her with that was enough to garner not one but three thank yous and a ridiculous amount of exclamation points?"

"Exclamation points? Do you know how ridiculous you sound right now?"

Another reprimand. But this one doesn't have the same effect as the last because knowing Brian has given Noelle support he's denied me has brought the boldness back. This time it's bolstered by an anger I never allow myself to fully access with Brian because I'm always skeptical of its validity and don't want to be accused of overreacting. This time any worries about that are overridden by the need to, for once, feel my feelings as they are, no filtering or minimizing.

"No, but I know that this is exactly how you sound when you're deflecting. Tell me what you did for her, Brian. Tell me how you went out of your way to make her dreams come true after spending nearly a decade shitting all over mine."

Fury lines every word so they fall off of my tongue and land like heavy lashes across the side of his face, caressing the throbbing muscle telegraphing his annoyance and demanding me to stop. Only, I can't stop because I want to know. No, I *need* to know because the part of me that's always just accepted that Brian comes from a long line of lawyers and other traditional careers and doesn't understand or value creativity, needs to know if it's actually creativity that's been disregarded and devalued by my life partner or just me.

Brian shakes his head. "I won't talk to you when you're like this. You know that."

"You're right. I do know. I know you hate it when I question you, when I refuse to comply, when I dare to have a thought or opinion that's contrary to yours. You hate when I push you, when I challenge you, when I want something you haven't given me permission to want or need something you don't feel ready to give. You—" I pause, catching my breath and swiping away angry, frustrated tears as another realization hits me. It's a simple truth really, but perhaps the most heartbreaking of the night. *"You don't like me."*

I shudder as the words leave me. The frigid, bleak reality settling around my shoulders as Brian rolls his eyes. "You're my wife, Grayson, of course I like you."

"No, you don't. You like the version of me you've trained me to be. The meek and quiet girl who's just grateful to have her life linked with yours, who agrees with whatever you say and gives up everything to make you happy. But that's not me, Brian. That person only exists around you. Have you ever realized that?"

Probably not because I'm just now realizing it myself. Just now allowing myself to acknowledge the disparity between who I am with him and who I am with and to everyone else.

He brings one hand up to his face, using his thumb and forefinger to pinch the bridge of his nose. "Let's table this subject for tonight. We've both had too much to drink."

"I'm sober as a judge, and I want to talk now."

It's rare for me to bring the pushy, bold, take no bullshit, side of me out around Brian, but I'm glad that she's here now, owning this moment, guiding me through this terrifying conversation that I know will end badly.

"Fine." Brian shifts in his seat, angling his body towards me. We're only a few minutes from home, and I can't shake the feeling that we're going to return to the house we've shared for six years a completely different couple than when we left it. "You want to talk? Let's talk. Noelle's business was in trouble, so I stepped in to help her. She needed a cash infusion, so I wired her the funds and promised to set her up with some of my contacts to help her get things back on track. The text messages that have you in such an uproar were simply her thanking me for helping her out. Now, if helping a friend in need makes me some kind of monster in your eyes, then I guess I'm a monster."

With his monologue finished, he leans back against the door and crosses his arms, wide eyes imploring me to continue this line of questioning now that he's painted himself out to be the victim in all of this. I cross my arms too, mirroring his posture.

"I don't think that makes you a monster, Brian." A smug smile tugs at the corners of his mouth, and I know he thinks he's got me. I let him sit with that lie for a second longer before I destroy it with my words. "You're a monster for a million different reasons. You're a monster for helping your friend out and refusing to support your wife in her pursuit of the same endeavor."

"Noelle actually has a business plan. You have an expired website domain, social media accounts you haven't touched in years, and an email list that's gone cold."

My gut clenches at the ugliness of his words, but I don't let it stop me from responding. "You're a monster for talking me into giving up a business I loved and then throwing its carcass in my face as some kind of proof for why your ex-girlfriend is more deserving of your support and resources than I am."

"You agreed to give up the business so we could start a family, Grayson. Don't make it seem like it was all my idea."

"You're a monster for insisting that stress from the business is the reason I was struggling to get pregnant, even though the fertility doctor told you months prior that your low sperm count was the actual culprit."

His eyes narrow into slits and his mouth drops open like he wants to say something, but no words come out.

"Brian, you're a monster because you married me when you knew I wasn't who you wanted, because you made it your mission to crush me under the weight of your expectations and punished me for turning into dust. You're a monster because you have never liked me, which means you could never really love me. Not in how I deserve."

The quiet whine of the brakes and a subtle jerk of the car lets me know that we've made it to our destination, and just as I suspected, Brian and I are not returning home the same people we were before. And maybe the change is just with me, but that's enough. It's enough to shake the foundation of who we are, enough to send me flying out of the car and into the house, straight to my closet where I pack a small bag of essentials while Brian follows me around and tries to talk me out of going.

He makes his final plea when I'm standing on the threshold of the front door, keys in hand, fear on one shoulder, hope on the other, and a lightness in my heart that makes no sense considering I'm about to walk away from the supposed love of my life.

"Do you actually think this little tantrum is going to work, Grayson? You think you're going to force my hand and make me take the money back from Noelle?" He reaches up and grips my chin, forcing me to look at him, to watch the ugly sneer curling his lips. "You think you're going to last a single day out there in the world without me? I give it a week, and then you'll be back. You're going to come crawling back to me."

And with that, he releases me, stepping back to study my face and posture, to see if his words have done anything to curb my desire to walk out the door and leave him behind. His shoulders sag a bit when he realizes they haven't, and for the first time tonight I smile an actual smile.

"No, Brian, I don't think I will."

2

GRAYSON

A Year Later

"GET YO SHIT! GET YO SHIT AND GET OUT!" My mother's voice joins with her sisters', blending into a disharmonious chorus that has me and my cousins— Chantel, A'ja and Kendra—taking one look at each other and dissolving into a fit of laughter on the floor at our mothers' feet.

We're all huddled in the living room of the home we grew up in. The modest one-story ranch-style house built from bricks laid by our great-grandfather's hands has been the site of many a core memory for myself and all the women in the room with me.

When I was little, it was my Grandma Belle's house. A place where sleepovers happened every weekend and family dinners were a regular occurrence. I took my prom pictures in the corner of this very living room because Aunt Marcel had made Chantel, her only daughter, and the oldest of us four cousins, do so the year before, and I wanted to be just like her. When Aunt Nita brought A'ja home from the hospital, this was her first stop. I stood behind the same couch the matriarchs of my family are curled up on right now, watching as Kendra held her baby sister for the first time.

This place was, and has always been, home for me, which is why it was the only place I thought to go when I left Brian a year ago. Even though it was late and I hadn't called ahead, my mom didn't bat an eye when I climbed into her bed, still wearing that stupidly expensive dress and the uncomfortable heels, clutching my keys like at any moment I might get up and bolt, running back to him like he said I would. No, she just wrapped her arms around me, kissed the top of my head and said, "It's about damn time," like she'd been waiting for forever for me to leave him.

Apparently she had.

Apparently *everybody* had.

"I still think you need to go back to the house and do that to Brian's shit," A'ja says when we've all recovered, chucking her chin toward the television where Angela Basset is now setting her husband's entire closet of designer shoes and clothing on fire inside his car.

"And get arrested?" Chantel asks at the same time Kendra claps her hands and says, "Ohh, yes, let's do it."

The wildly varying responses set us off again, and this time our mothers join in. We take a full minute to get it all out, and by the time we're done, my sides hurt. They always seem to be cursed with this joyous kind of ache when I'm around my family, when I'm embraced in their love and acceptance.

"Seriously, though," Kendra says, gripping her sides as a sly smile curves her lips. "We could do it if you wanted to. I mean, it's not like he wouldn't deserve it."

"Don't listen to her, Gray," my mother chides, taking a long sip from the glass of blood red wine in her hand. "Nothing good will come from you going over to that man's house."

Even though I'm the one that left, the one that walked away and used every fiber of strength in my body not to look back, it still stings when I hear things that once belonged to Brian and I referred to as just his. Our home used to be Brian and Grayson's house, and now it's just his.

It's been twelve months and a day since I stepped foot inside of the sprawling two story Craftsman where we planned to raise a family. Six since the last time I drove by, just to see if my old life missed me as much as I sometimes missed it. Well, not it exactly, but the illusion of it. The love built from a facade, and the lies I told myself to uphold it. The comfort of the familiar, even when familiar hurts, even when it makes you bleed as it breaks you.

"I know, Ma," I assure her, solidifying it with a serious glance tossed over my shoulder. She smiles, proud of me, of my strength, of the resolve I can only hold on to because of her.

"It's too late for her to act a fool on him anyway," Aunt Nita announces to the room. "You should have played your crazy card the first time he played his. The first time your Uncle Nate tried to get buck with me, I wanted to kill him, but I didn't."

Kendra spins around, eyeing her mother with keen interest. It's not often that Aunt Nita talks about her late husband and the father of both of her daughters, so when she mentions him—even when it sounds like it's about to be a crazy story—we all tune in.

"What'd you do, Mommy?" A'ja asks, turning to rest her chin on Aunt Nita's knee.

"Oh, Lord," Aunt Marcel says through lips twisted with disapproval. It never ceases to amaze me how much she and Chantel look alike when they're judging one of us. "Don't tell me this is the story where—"

"Shhh, Cel! Let Nita tell it," my mom says, fighting back a giggle.

"Lottie loves this story," Aunt Nita tells us, sharing a conspiratorial look with my mom who doesn't bat an eye at the shortened, almost infantilizing version of her name. No one else in the world, not even my dad, would dare call her anything but Charlotte, but to my aunts she's always been, and will always be, Lottie.

"I really do," Mom agrees.

Kendra taps her mother's leg impatiently. "Well, tell us so we can love it too!"

"And find a way to use it on one of the many men on your roster," Chantel adds in the signature soft but cutting tone she uses when she's judging one of us but trying really hard not to let it show.

A'ja and Kendra high five and laugh. "Damn right," they say in unison, taking no offense to our uptight cousin's expression of disapproval.

"Y'all gone listen, or you just gone keep talking among yourselves?" Aunt Nita asks, splitting an impatient look between her daughters, me and Chantel.

My lips part as I prepare to let her know I wasn't the one talking, but Chantel places a hand on my knee and shakes her head, the cinnamon brown eyes we all inherited from our mothers pleading with me not to derail the conversation once more. I trap my pointless protest behind a smile that I pair with a nod of my head to let Aunt Nita know she can begin her story.

"Nate and I had just gotten married, and I was a few months pregnant with you, Kendra, when I found out he slept with some hussy who worked in the front office of the factory. He said it was a one-time thing and apologized, even offered to find a different job, but I wasn't about to have his ass out of work when we were about to have another mouth to feed." She pauses and holds her hand out, gesturing to her glass on the coffee table. "Grayson, hand me my wine, please." I pluck the still full goblet up and place it in her outstretched hand. "Thank you, baby."

"You're welcome."

After taking a few sips, Aunt Nita clutches the glass between her palms and continues. "Months went by, and Nate thought we were back to normal. Hell, I did too, but the closer I got to my due date, the more I started to think that I had to make sure he never pulled no shit like that on me again because I wasn't gone raise my child in no dysfunctional family. So a few weeks before I had Kendra, I called Nate while he was at work and told him his mama had died."

Every mouth in the room drops, except, of course, for the older women who've already heard this story. We're all quiet for a moment while Aunt Nita lets us absorb the fact that she'd spoken death over a woman who, still to this day, is very much alive.

"Mommy!" Kendra shrieks, slapping her hand over mouth. "What in the world?"

"That's some unhinged shit for real," A'ja cackles.

Chantel and Aunt Marcel both hum their agreement while my mother falls over giggling. "Nate got a speeding ticket racing over to his mama's house to meet you. He was so damn mad."

"You had him meet you at her house?" I ask, voice laced with incredulity. I've always known my aunt was a hot mess, but I didn't think her crazy ran *this* deep.

"Sure did," Aunt Nita laughs. "I met him outside, though. He was crying like a baby, and I'm just standing there with my big ole belly trying to get him calm so he can listen to me. It took forever," she says, rolling her eyes.

"You told him his mama was dead, Nita," Aunt Marcel chides. "Of course, he was inconsolable."

Aunt Nita waves her off. "Anyway, when I finally got him calm, I told him that his mama was very much alive, but I wanted him to remember this feeling, to hold on to that grief and sadness because if he ever stepped out on me again I was going to make that feeling permanent."

"You threatened to kill Nana?!"

A'ja's jaw is damn near on the floor, and her eyes are stretched wide, pupils dancing with a mix between horror and admiration.

"I sure did, and it worked too. Up until the day he died, your daddy never strayed from my bed again."

The ending to the most unhinged story is punctuated by the ringing of the doorbell. Since I'm closest to the door, I hop up and walk the short distance to the front of the house. The front door is open, letting in the last bit of daylight through the glass screen door, and there's a man I don't know standing on the porch. He looks normal enough, dressed in dark jeans and a sweater with a heavy trench to keep out the cold, and leather gloves on his hands. However, he's still a stranger, so I don't open the screen door completely.

"Can I help you?"

"Are you Grayson Hart?" he asks, looking me over with eyes that tell me he already knows the answer to that question.

"Yes."

Upon my confirmation, he brings up his right hand and extends it, holding out the thin manila envelope I apparently missed on my cursory inspection of his person. On instinct, I reach out and take it.

"You've been served."

3

XAVIER

She doesn't want to be here.

That much is clear to me by the way her gaze keeps flitting around the room. Auburn eyes roaming over the walls covered with my degrees, various awards for professionalism and superior litigation, and commendations for philanthropy thanks to the pro-bono cases that make up a small portion of my annual case load.

Grayson Hart won't fall into that category.

She strode into my office, a quiet storm of tightly reined emotion in a black pantsuit that clung to her curved frame, and slid a check for my full retainer onto my desk. Then she sat down, crossed her legs, and deflated right in front of me. All the bravado, confidence, and purpose melting out of her body in a slow, painful leak that would have broken my heart if I had one.

Fortunately, ten years of this work has relieved me of the organ. Or maybe I surrendered it, knowing I couldn't rise to the top of my field and become the youngest named partner in the history of my firm if I held on to it. Whatever the case, my ability to place my feelings in a box serves me well, allowing me to leave space for the clients who come to me, hoping I'll be their saving grace.

Clearing my throat, I slide the check to the side and pull out a fresh legal pad to take notes. Grayson's eyes follow my movements, and even out of the corner of my eye, I can see her bracing herself. She knows what comes next, and she's dreading it. The talking, the tears, the vulnerability of divulging the intimate details of her life. But at the same time, she knows, just like I do, that she doesn't have a choice.

"Alright, Mrs. Hart—"

"Grayson," she insists, her voice flat and dejected. "You can call me Grayson."

"Grayson," I repeat, nodding as I give her a reassuring smile that does nothing to dispel the tension that's settled itself in her muscles. "Tell me how we got here."

She swallows and presses her lips together. I can see her trying to figure out where to start. That's the thing about marriages. When they fall apart, you look back and realize that the breakdown started long before *the moment*. Before the loud betrayal or the quiet resentment that finally made you call it quits. You look at the waste of your union and find that there are a million little threads attached to it, weaving their way through it, causing cracks and rifts that rendered it irreparable.

And when you're sitting down with someone like me, someone who's entire job is to exploit those cracks and ensure you're able to create something out of the wreckage, then it all starts to feel like too much. Too much information to sort through, too much pain to process, too much everything.

Grayson has been silent for a full minute now, and I stay in it with her, letting her process. Most attorneys would have jumped in at this point, prodding her with questions and assumptions about what led her here, but I don't do that because she has to lead. She has to speak. She has to tell me what's important, and that only happens if I wait patiently to find out where she starts her story.

"I was a fashion designer," she says finally. "I mean, I am—" she pauses, unsure if she can claim the title anymore. While she finds her words, I write 'fashion designer' on the top line of my paper. "When I was a junior in college, I started a plus size clothing brand called Elysian. This is actually one of my pieces."

She gestures at the luxurious black fabric clinging to her crossed legs, and I study it with renewed interest. It's a simple piece, classic and stylish, with a thick strip of black satin covering the seam running down her leg. The black blazer and vest she's paired it with both have the same satin accents, which means they were made to be worn together. The impeccable fit lets me know this suit was made with her exact dimensions in mind. It fits like a glove.

"It's beautiful."

"Thank you." The beginning of a smile plays at the corner of her lips, but she shuts it down, giving in to the cloud of sadness that clearly hovers above any thoughts of her work now. "Anyway," she continues, "I started the brand, and it was a small, but successful operation. At first it was just me in my dorm room killing myself because I was sewing everything by hand, but in the end I had a team and a warehouse and had gone through all the trouble of finding manufacturers with ethical practices to outsource production. In any given month, we were doing sixty to eighty thousand in sales."

A low whistle passes between my lips as I write that number down, knowing that it matters to Grayson now and will matter to me later. This time she allows the smile to curve her lips, and I soak in the pride shining in her eyes.

"That's impressive," I tell her, and she nods like she doesn't believe I'm being genuine.

"About six months after we got married, Brian decided it was time for us to start a family," she goes on, not acknowledging my comment. "Even though I've always wanted to be a mom, I was hesitant. I still had so much I wanted to do before I gave up this entire part of myself to a child, but Brian was insistent. He said we'd be able to balance it all, to make it work. I believed him, and we started trying."

She grimaces. "Getting pregnant isn't nearly as easy as you'd think. We ended up going to a fertility specialist, and of course they always warn you about stress and alcohol and all the things the person with the uterus should give up in order to conceive. Naturally, Brian clung to those things, holding them up as the reason the tests came back negative every month." Her tongue escapes her mouth, passing over her full lips in a quick swipe before she resumes speaking.

"Eventually, he used them to talk me into shutting down Elysian. He said the stress was too much for me, and I might as well say goodbye to it now because when the baby came, I wouldn't want to do it anymore, anyway. What he failed to mention, even after I caved to his demands, is that his low sperm count was actually the issue."

I'd paused my note taking to take a sip of my coffee, so when Grayson drops that little bomb, I damn near choke on the scorching hot liquid. Her eyes stretch wide with surprise when a sharp bark leaves me, and I slap a hand firmly on my chest in quick succession to silence it.

"Are you okay?"

Setting the mug back down, I nod. "Yeah, I'm good. Sorry. Did you, uh," I cough again, trying to clear out the wobble in my voice that's as much a result of the choking as it is of the laugh I'm holding in. "Sorry. Did you and your husband end up conceiving?"

"No."

I write that down and study her face. "Is that the reason you left him?"

"How did you know I'm the one that left?"

Almost on instinct, my eyes go to her hands, tracing over the knuckles of her bare ring fingers. Grayson's right hand comes up, forming a protective layer over the left. "Oh," she says, biting her lip.

"Yeah, in my experience, women don't take off their ring unless they've given up all hope, and they don't usually feel that way unless they're the ones who pulled the plug."

"I guess that makes sense, but no, that's not why I left him. Like I said before, kids have always been a later thing for me. I left him because I got tired of being married to someone who didn't like me," she scoffs and rolls her eyes. "God, that sounds so stupid, doesn't it? Every time I say, it sounds worse than before."

"No, Grayson, I don't think that sounds stupid at all. If someone doesn't like you, then they won't ever know how to love you," I tell her, my voice tender, warm in a way it never is when I speak to clients because I only ever want them to see me as the cold, relentless shark who'll dismember and eat everything in its path to get them what they want.

Grayson seems to appreciate the tenderness, though. She blooms underneath my gentle timbre. Trust and vulnerability unfurls in her gaze, landing like flower petals at my feet. She's so captivating like this, all open and unguarded, free from whatever burdens and trauma her ex left her to carry. I can't look away even though I know I should. Even though I know this amount of eye contact, held for *this* long is weird and borderline inappropriate.

It doesn't help that Grayson is right there with me, holding us in this moment, both of us refusing to set the other free.

"I've made copies of the pre and post-nuptial agreements and gotten the official filings from the court," Mara, my paralegal, announces as she walks into the room without knocking, breaking our shared trance.

Tearing my eyes away from Grayson, I accept the folders from Mara and open them up. "Thank you."

"No worries. Grayson, are you sure I can't get you something? Water, soda, a cappuccino? Xavier has these amazing espresso beans in the back of the freezer in the break room. I'm sure he wouldn't mind if I ground some up for you."

Mara's enthusiasm and charm make Grayson laugh. It's not loud, and it doesn't last long, but it's a delightful sound that I wouldn't mind hearing again.

"No," she replies. "I think I'm okay."

"Alright, but if you change your mind, let me know."

"I will."

Mara turns to me, brows raised. "Need anything else?"

"No, I'm good. Go to lunch and take the entire hour, please."

Mara salutes me and leaves just as quickly as she came, making no promises to honor my request for her to use the entirety of her break. I tell her all the time that she works too hard, but she always meets my comments with a smart remark about how she learned all about uneven work/life balance from me.

Once we're alone again, I take control of the conversation, moving us to the more technical, less emotional part of the meeting. This is where I thrive, in the certainty of black letters on white pages that make up clauses and terms and agreements. Because when it's all said and done, that's really all marriage comes down to.

I pick my pen up again, and Grayson sits up straighter, her spine turning rigid at the sight of my serious expression. "Let's establish a timeline. When did you leave Brian?"

"Christmas Eve, last year."

"And after that point, did you ever have contact with Brian or return to the marital home?"

Grayson shakes her head, shifting in her seat. "No. I didn't want to see or talk to him because I didn't want to risk being talked into coming back to him. I wanted a clean break, and I figured that would go a long way towards meeting the one year separation period required for a no-fault divorce."

My brows lift in surprise, shocked that she knows the term. "So you were planning to file for divorce and cite irreconcilable differences?"

"Yes, I thought that would be best. Brian can be vindictive when he feels like he's being challenged, and I don't want to fight with him."

Glancing down, I study the first page of the divorce petition, finding the line that specifies Brian's complaint. "It looks like he wants to fight with you, though. He's saying that you deserted him."

"I know, but that's not a thing, right? Like he can't claim desertion when I'm not the sole breadwinner, and he's not dependent on me for anything, can he?"

I turn the page, finding the beginnings of a meticulously kept record of un-returned calls and emails and texts, and look back up at Grayson. "Unfortunately, he can. Desertion isn't only meant for a man who leaves his wife and kids destitute while he goes off and starts a new life. A good lawyer can make a case for it based on you moving out without Brian's consent and having no plans to return to the marital home. All of which you've just admitted to."

"But that was for the separation period," she says, her tone harsh, laced with a volatile reaction to the unfairness of the situation. She thought she was doing things the right way, that this would all be simple, but her husband is determined to make it anything but. The slick bastard started the clock as soon as she walked out on him, knowing how he wanted this to go all along. If it wasn't so fucked up, I'd probably admire the guy for having the wherewithal to play the long game.

"So I'm going to have to fight him?"

"You don't have to do anything you don't want to do, Grayson. You can admit fault, sign the papers and be done with him forever. However, according to the terms of the post-nuptial agreement you signed after closing your business, that means you won't be eligible to receive the funds in the trust Brian has been paying your projected earnings into for the last five years."

Her mouth drops open. "What? Brian said that money would be mine no matter what! He knows I need it to rebuild Elysian, to rebuild my life."

I shake my head, fighting the urge to tell her that's the point. That her husband doesn't want her to recover from leaving him, that he wants her permanently devastated by the dissolution of their union. "I understand, but that's not what your post-nup says."

Grayson's shoulders sag, and she sinks back into her seat with tears glossing over her eyes. My chest tightens as I watch one escape, slipping out of the corner of her eye and sliding over the roundness of her cheeks. Leaning forward, I reach for the box of tissues I keep on the edge of my desk, plucking one up and handing it to her. I've done this a million times, handed a client a tissue, reassured them they weren't stupid or naïve and that everything would be okay. It's always been enough, but this time I wish that I could do more. That I could give more. That I could *be* more for her.

"I'm sorry, Grayson," I say softly, knowing the words aren't enough.

"Don't be. I should have known he would do something like this. He's spent his entire life watching his father do nasty, underhanded shit for his clients, so I shouldn't be surprised, especially not after the stunt he pulled with the other lawyers."

My brow furrows. "Other lawyers?"

Grayson dabs at her cheek with the tissue and nods. "I met with several other attorneys before I came here. They all said they couldn't represent me because it would be a conflict of interest. When I asked them what they meant, they explained Brian had already retained their services." She shakes her head, incredulity skating across her features. "What kind of person does that?"

"A smart one," I answer begrudgingly, making note of the successful deployment of the unethical tactic of "conflicting out" other lawyers. Most people wouldn't even think to do it, and even less could afford to pull it off. That Grayson's husband has done both tells me we're in for a fight. When I look up again, her eyes are on my face. She's watching me closely, wariness written in every line of her expression.

"You sound impressed," she says.

"Not impressed. Excited."

"Excited?"

Her brows crinkle with surprise and maybe a bit of confusion, which pulls my lips up into a grin that bares all of my teeth. "Yes, Grayson, excited. Brian and his team are clearly willing to play dirty, so I'm going to get in the mud with them and make them wish they'd kept their hands clean."

She nods, but I can tell by the continued dullness behind her eyes that she doesn't believe me yet. That's okay. Because once she sees me eviscerate her husband during depositions, lay waste to the pre and post nuptial agreements I'm sure he strong armed her into signing, and file complaints with the Ethics Advisory Committee on every lawyer involved in his little conflict scheme, she will.

My heart pumps with anticipation, blood coursing through my veins at an accelerated rate at the mere thought of a good fight. "You said Brian grew up watching his father do stuff like this for clients. Is he a lawyer?"

"Yes. Brian is a lawyer as well. His whole family is full of lawyers. All of them little minions doing Bernard Lucas' bidding."

I'm halfway through writing her father-in-law's name down when all the pieces fall together. The legal savvy, the dirty tactics, the financial means to pull it off. I drop my pen and look at Grayson, giving her my full attention, making sure this means what I think it does.

"Your husband is Brian Lucas?"

Brian is the oldest son and protégé of Bernard Lucas, a well known, well-respected powerhouse in the world of family law and a close friend of the other named partners here at Savage, Colfax, Kaplan and Allen. We met in law school and became fast enemies because I was the only person in our cohort who refused to kiss his ass. Today, I wouldn't consider him an enemy, just a random asshole I take extreme pleasure in beating in court whenever I get the chance.

"Yes, is that going to be a problem for you?" Grayson asks, her eyes already glazed over with disappointment, expecting me to fold under the weight of her husband's last name. I can see that this situation has taken a toll on her. That navigating the early stages of this divorce on her own has left her discouraged and afraid that she's going to have to cave to Brian's demands and be just another person crushed by the machine that is the Lucas family.

I'm certain that's what Brian and his father are expecting her to do. Just like I'm certain they weren't expecting her to come to me. It's almost laughable how they counted me out, not even trying to retain my services, leaving me open and available to take Grayson's case, to get her more than her fair share of everything he has.

"No." I shake my head for emphasis, another teeth baring grin tugging at my lips. "That won't be a problem for me."

Relief smooths the creases in her forehead. "Okay." She goes quiet for a moment and then sighs. "I can't believe I'm going to war with Brian."

"*You're* not going to war with Brian, Grayson," I toss back, my tone assertive and riddled with certainty. "*We* are, and I can promise you, we're going to win."

4

GRAYSON

No matter how old I get, I will never pass up an opportunity to lie in my mom's bed, especially if she's just gotten out of it to get ready for work. There's something so satisfying about sinking into the spot in the mattress still warm from her body, laying my head on a pillow that still smells like the oil she brushes through her hair before she wraps it up at night, watching her put on her clothes for the day and weighing in on what shoes she should wear.

Since moving back in with her, I've done it often, happy to reenact the summer mornings of my childhood when I'd receive a kiss on the forehead and a reminder not to stay in bed all day before she rushed out the door, leaving me to do exactly that.

Back then, Mom thought it was cute to come home and find me napping in her bed, cartoons on her TV and several bowls of cereal on her nightstand beside a pile of books, but these days she's less thrilled about it.

"When are you going back to work?" she asks as soon as she crosses the threshold into her bedroom, heels in one hand while the other is perched on her hip. She's almost sixty years old, but she's still got that curvy, slim figure that used to make my dad refer to her as a Coke bottle.

"Jax told me to take as much time as I need," I answer from the comfort of her spot in the bed. Convincing Brian to let me go back to work in some capacity had been a challenge after we pressed pause on trying to get pregnant, but he'd agreed eagerly after he met Jax. Something about hearing my job description in a man's voice made him so very agreeable. Now that I look back on it, I realize how problematic that was. I guess that's why they say hindsight is twenty-twenty.

Mom tuts her disapproval as she makes her way over to her closet to grab a change of clothes before disappearing into her bathroom. I know her post-work routine like the back of my hand, so it doesn't surprise me to hear the shower running shortly after the door closes, just like it doesn't surprise me when she jumps right back into our conversation when she emerges fifteen minutes later.

"Jax gave you time off so you could focus on Elysian, not mope around in my bed all day."

My stomach lurches, my body revolting at being called out in such a matter-of-fact way. Even though my mother is right, it's still hard to hear, to know that I'm failing so epically at the thing I want most in the world. And it's not even the designing or the creating part that's hard—because I never stopped sketching and sewing—it's everything else.

The social media platforms I don't know how to show up on, the would be customers I don't know how to connect with anymore.

It's the empty, black squares on an app all about pictures and aesthetics and the silence underneath the few posts I've felt brave enough to put up.

It's the pity likes from my mom, cousins, aunts and Amina—Jax's wife.

It's the website with no pictures of me or my products and no copy to explain who I am or what the brand means to me.

It's Brian's voice in my head telling me I'll fail, and the crippling fear that he's right.

"I'm trying. It's just hard when—"

She waves a hand in the air, cutting my sentence in half. "No, no, no. I don't want to hear none of that. You have that strong, sexy, extremely intelligent lawyer in your corner taking care of everything on the divorce front, putting in all the work to sever ties with your old life. It's up to you to lay the groundwork for your new one."

The eye roll at her description of Xavier is unintentional, but it doesn't stop her from swatting me on the hip as she urges me towards the center of the bed so she can sit on the edge and put her lotion on.

"You're right," I tell her, sitting up and resting my back against the headboard.

"Of course I am, baby."

"And so humble too," I muse.

"I don't need to be humble when I have correctness on my side."

"Now that's a word, auntie," a voice says from the door. Mom and I both look up to find Kendra strutting into the room with a wide grin on her face.

I scoot to the edge of the bed and meet her in the middle of the floor for a hug. "What are you doing here, Ken?"

She squeezes me long and hard before pulling back. "Lottie Dottie said you needed a little pick me up, so the girls and I decided to come through."

"And thank God you did. I don't think this girl has left my bed all day," Mom says from behind us. One glance back reveals her on all fours in the center of the king sized bed, starting at the furthest corner to wrench the sheets free from the mattress.

Choosing not to engage with my mother's dramatics, I turn back to Kendra. "I appreciate y'all coming to cheer me up, but I don't feel like going out or anything."

"Who said anything about going out?" Kendra asks as she grabs my hand, leading me out of the room. I follow her into the dining room on hesitant feet and smile when I see Chantel and A'ja gathered around the table with their laptops, snacks and glasses full of wine in the center. Kendra leads me to the head of the table and forces me to sit down.

"What is all this?"

Chantel passes me a glass of wine and smiles. "The first official Elysian Re-Launch planning meeting."

"The what?!"

A'ja rolls her eyes, her fingers typing away on a laptop she soon spins around the places in front of me. "Girl, you heard what she said. Now log me into your Insta, so I can see what you been in here doing."

I don't protest. I mean, how can I when I have three people here and willing to help me with all the stuff that's been stressing me out for the last few weeks? After I log A'ja into my socials, I open my laptop, which had been waiting on the table for me, and give Chantel access to my bank accounts, so she can create a budget for me to produce a small collection to launch at the event Kendra is apparently planning.

"Jax says you can use the event space at the back of Refrain, and he's going to make sure his friends Mallory and Sloane are there. Apparently, Mallory works for some big venture capital firm and her entire job is finding small businesses for them to fund and making sure they're successful afterwards. She's also a plus sized girl, so maybe you can gift her a piece from the collection."

Chantel and A'ja hum their agreement while I make note of the suggestion. "That's a great idea, Ken." I look around the table, at all of the work we've put in, in just a few hours. "These are all great ideas. Thank you guys for doing this."

My voice breaks as tears begin to crowd my vision. Suddenly, there are three sets of arms around me, squeezing tight, and three sets of lips murmuring soft assurances in my ear, making me believe that it'll all be okay. When I'm safely on the other side of my little breakdown, everyone returns to their seats, and we get back to work.

"Have you heard anything from your lawyer?" Chantel asks after a while, glancing at me over the blue light glasses she has perched on her nose.

I use the pencil in my hand to scratch out the sketch I was just working on and then flip the page to start new. "He called yesterday."

A shiver runs down my spine at the thought of Xavier Allen's phone voice. It's the perfect balance of gruff and tender, profession- alism stained with sin. The man could be a phone sex operator if he wanted to.

A'ja cuts her eye at me. "And?"

"And apparently I have to go to court tomorrow."

"Tomorrow?!" Kendra shrieks. "Why didn't you say anything before now? I could have taken the day off."

"Because I didn't want you to take the day off. It's just a hearing. Xavier says we'll be in and out because it'll only take the judge a few minutes to rule on the temporary orders."

Kendra arches a brow. "What's that?"

Leaning back in my chair, I try to remember Xavier's exact wording when he explained it to me yesterday. "Orders that address issues that need to be handled immediately while the divorce is still pending. Usually stuff like child support, custody or spousal support."

Chantel picks up her wine and takes a sip. "But you guys don't have kids, and you said your post-nup prevents you from collecting spousal support, so what else is there to handle?"

"Property," A'ja offers, plucking a grape from the charcuterie board in the center of the table and popping it into her mouth.

I nod, bracing myself for the hell my cousins are going to raise when they hear the rest of the story. "Yep, apparently Brian wants the judge to order me to stay away from the house—"

"You've already been doing that," Kendra says.

"And," I continue, "he wants me to give back my car."

The white Audi Q3 was Brian's gift to me for our sixth wedding anniversary. I'd never put much stock into vehicles, only really caring about their ability to get me from point A to point B, but over time I've come to love the SUV. It also happens to be my only source of transportation, so losing it would probably mean having to quit my job since Jax is primarily operating out of his restaurant in New Haven, and I'm now an hour away, in the outskirts of Fairview. Brian, of course, knows all of this, which is why he's trying to force me to give it back.

All three of my cousins show signs of disgust and outrage, but it's A'ja who voices it first. Her button nose is wrinkled with fury. "What a fucking asshole. I hope he catches a cold in his balls and dies of testicular pneumonia."

"Pretty sure that's not a real thing." Chantel laughs before adding, "But I get the sentiment."

"Is Xavier going to fight it?"

Kendra, the sweetest and most considerate of all of us, looks so concerned, and I can see the wheels in her brain turning, probably trying to figure out how she can help if I end up losing my car. Before she can offer her vehicle or start talking to me about joint car schedules that include picking up and dropping off her seven-year-old son, Crew, I place a reassuring hand over hers.

"Yes, and he's confident he'll be able to get it thrown out."

"Good," she whispers, relieved. "I'm so glad you have someone like him protecting you from that abusive asshole, Brian."

I pull a face, something about the phrasing hitting me all wrong. "Brian is a lot of things, Ken, but abusive isn't one of them."

The entire room goes quiet. Chantel's fingers pause on the keyboard of her laptop. A'ja stops the music on her phone. Even the damn heat turns off, leaving us in the awkward silence that follows my statement. I look around at all of them, confused by their confusion.

"What?" I ask, genuinely curious. "I really don't think abusive is the right word. I mean, it's not like he hit me or anything."

"Emotional abuse is still abuse, Gray," A'ja says, her tone soft, her eyes pitying. "You know that, right?"

"Of course, I know that. I just—" I stop, looking around the table, seeing a rebuttal to my unspoken statement in all of their eyes. "I wasn't *abused*."

The words leave my mouth, but there's no conviction in my tone. No certainty to lay the declaration on top of, just doubt. Just questions and the painful re-framing of every moment I shared with my husband. Every critique presented as a helpful suggestion. Every discussion rigged for an outcome in his favor. Every discouragement phrased as a question about my capacity. Every cut down growing bolder and bolder until he didn't even have to hide them anymore, until I just accepted that whatever he gave me was what I deserved.

I slap a hand over my mouth as my mind and body reel, processing this new reality in a painful span of seconds that feels like it lasts for an eternity. I don't realize that I'm sobbing until the hard press of my mom's arms around my shoulders brings me back to my body, to the trail of wetness running from my eyes, over my cheeks and down my neck. I don't know where she came from, but I'm glad she's here.

"Shhh," she coos, rocking me back and forth. "You're okay, baby girl. You're okay."

"I stayed," I sob, the words coming out broken. "He hurt me. He kept hurting me, and I just stayed. Why would I do that, Mommy? How could I be so stupid?"

"You're not stupid, Grayson. *You're brave.* You're so brave, baby. You got yourself out of there." She peppers kisses over my temple and wet cheeks. "You are so brave, and I'm so very proud of you."

My mother's words are the coat of armor I wear to court the next day. They keep me insulated from everything happening around me. From Xavier sitting next to me at the table in front of the judge's bench, from the argument Brian's lawyer, a sleazy looking bald man named Monty Barnes, makes for me to return the car, from the judge's ruling in my favor.

Nothing goes out, and nothing comes in.

That is until Brian corners me in the parking lot outside of the courtroom. I'd left Xavier behind as soon as the hearing was over, ignoring his offer to walk me to my car. As soon as Brian catches up to me, I regret that decision.

He grabs me by the arm, touching me like he still has a right to, and forces me to spin around and face him. His cheeks are tinted red from the anger coursing through him and the harsh bite of the wind whipping around us. I snatch away, pulling my coat in tighter around me as I stare at him, wondering how I ever saw anything but a monster when I looked in his eyes.

"Out of all the attorneys you could have gone with, you decide to go with *him*?" he sneers, which makes me want to laugh. Xavier had said it would bother Brian to see us in court together because of their history. I didn't think I'd get to see that in action, but I guess I was wrong.

Brian isn't as tall as Xavier, but he's still taller than me, tall enough that I have to tip my head back to look up at him. He's handsome in a classic kind of way—I can still acknowledge that even though I know what he is now—but I'm not moved by his features like I once was.

"It's not like you left me a lot of choices, Brian."

A frown tugs down the corners of his mouth, telegraphing just how much he hates that I know exactly how dirty he's been playing since the beginning of this divorce. "Yeah, but you still should have gone with someone else. You know he only took this case to piss me off."

I tilt my head to the side, studying him. "You really believe that, don't you?"

He flounders for an answer, spending less than a second on formulating one before deciding to switch gears. "I don't get you, Grayson. You don't want me, but you want the car I bought you for our anniversary. Didn't anyone tell you that walking away from me meant walking away from everything with my name attached to it?"

"Didn't anyone tell you that speaking to my client without me present is inappropriate and highly unethical?"

The question comes from behind me, hitting my ears at the same time a set of warm, leather clad gloves cup my hip and gently, but forcefully, move me to the side. In seconds, I go from standing face to face with Brian to standing behind Xavier as he towers over us both, looking down at my soon to be ex-husband with a murderous scowl.

"Your *client* is my wife," Brian protests. He tries to sidestep the larger man to get to me, but Xavier isn't having it.

"Not for long," Xavier tosses back, stepping to the left when Brian does and forcing him back with a large hand on his chest. "Now get the fuck out of here before I report this little incident to the judge."

Wide, angry eyes pass over the two of us, and I don't know if Xavier feels the waves of outrage rolling off of Brian, but I do. As he walks away, I marvel at how obvious it all is now—the bitterness coursing through him, the hatred and malice—wondering if he was good at hiding it or if I was just adept at not seeing it.

"Are you okay?" Xavier asks, rounding on me when Brian is out of our sight. It's a clear, bitterly cold January day and what little sunlight there is has decided to play on the lines of his face. Normally, I don't call men beautiful, but that's always the word that comes to mind when

I'm in Xavier's presence, because no other word really does him justice. He has one of those faces that suggests his creation was a labor of love, a slow, intentional process that resulted in rugged, yet symmetrical, features that exist in perfect harmony with the oiled mahogany of his complexion and the deep, black waves that hug his scalp.

He runs a large hand over those waves, genuine concern in low, hooded eyes that spell bedroom, not courtroom.

"Grayson?"

I jolt, heat cresting on my cheeks at having been caught staring. "Yes, I'm fine. Sorry."

"Don't apologize. I saw him corner you. I figured he wouldn't take losing the hearing well, which is why I wanted to walk you to your car in the first place."

"Right. I'm sorry I didn't take you up on that. It won't happen again."

"Damn right it won't," he growls. "Because next time I won't ask."

The bite he pairs with that bark has heat trickling through my core, and I clench my thighs to quell the involuntary reaction, which only grows stronger when Xavier comes up beside me and puts his hand on the small of my back.

"Let's get you to your car."

We walk the short distance to my vehicle in silence, and I get the sense that Xavier is still fuming. It doesn't feel like he's angry with me so much as he is at the situation. I haven't known him for long, but I am learning his expressions. To recognize what he looks like when he's ready to sink his teeth into something—or someone—and destroy them.

And right now, that someone is Brian.

Once we're at my car, I unlock the door from my key fob, and Xavier opens it. His jaw is tense, but his eyes are soft as they pass over my features.

"I'm okay," I assure him.

He nods, running the hand not holding my door open over his chin. "I don't think I have to remind you of this after today, but you can't speak to Brian alone, Grayson. He'll take anything you say or do and twist it around for the good of his case, and I'm already struggling to find a strong angle for our counterclaim, as it is."

Most of our conversations of late have either been about this hearing or about the counterclaim. Xavier says we need something good, but real. He doesn't want it to be sensationalized or manipulated information meant to warp perception like the evidence Brian's built his case on. Before last night, I had no idea how to help him help me, but now, after the epiphany I had at the table surrounded by the women who love me and recognized the abuse before I did, I think I might.

I swallow past the lump in my throat, past the embarrassment and shame, and look Xavier square in the eye. "Do you think we can build a case around emotional abuse?"

5

XAVIER

When Grayson pitched the emotional abuse angle for our counterclaim, my stomach dropped. Not because I didn't think it would work, but because I knew it would.

Someone who's been in this business as long as I have, who came into it for the fucked up reasons I did, can spot the hallmarks of abuse from a mile away. And when you're really good, like I am, you can distinguish between the different types just by observing the person who survived it.

When it's physical, the client exhibits a heart breaking kind of hypervigilance, alarmingly aware of every move you make, flinching when you reach out to shake their hand, shrinking when you come near them to make themselves a smaller target.

When it's financial, it's more subtle. The client does odd things, like offering explanations you didn't ask for, and don't need, about every purchase, no matter how big or small. They berate themselves for buying a new outfit for court, call a cup of coffee a splurge and carry around cash to hide purchases from partners who monitor their bank accounts too closely.

And when it's emotional, the client wears the abuse like a second skin. It manifests in self-deprecating thoughts and nasty comments they aim at themselves and no one else. It lives behind their eyes, stealing light and joy as the abuser's words poison them from the inside out, shredding their self-esteem, robbing them of every morsel of their self-worth until they're nothing but an empty shell of internalized hatred and negativity.

The moment Grayson walked into my office, I knew she fell into the latter category. With any other client, I would have immediately latched on to that, skillfully, but maybe a little tactlessly, convincing them to use it in their counterclaim. With any other client, I wouldn't have spent days trying to find a new angle to spare them the pain of reliving the abuse. With any other client, I wouldn't have gone home sick to my stomach and flirting with the idea of murder on the day she sat down and told me the full story, raw and unfiltered in her recounting of the years of manipulation that started in high school when that fucking scumbag fucked her in secret but refused to love her out loud.

My hand turns into a fist at the thought, and a renewed sense of hatred for Brian Lucas surges through me. I want to destroy him, not just legally, because I will do that, but physically. No, biologically, I want to rid the planet of his existence, wipe his DNA from humanity's ledger, obliterate his essence from the cosmos so that when Grayson looks up at the sky, it's all new. An entire world for her to thrive in that's untouched by him. I close my eyes and push out a breath through my nose as I move forward in the short line for popcorn, exhaling all the anger I can't do anything with, and inhaling the soothing scent of melted butter and salt.

The movie theater on a random weekday in the middle of the afternoon is my favorite place to be when the thoughts in my head get to be too much. Lately, that's more often than not. Ever since seeing Brian towering over Grayson in the courthouse parking lot a few weeks ago, I've been here once a week, using popcorn and the guaranteed happily ever afters of movies I won't ever admit to watching to distract myself from the things out of my control. I had thought filing the counterclaim today would help quiet my mind, but I was wrong. As soon as Mara texted to say that everything had been submitted, my mind started to race. Thoughts of all the ways Brian might retaliate against Grayson making it impossible for me to focus for the rest of the day.

"I knew you'd be back," Jada, the theater employee who's always working when I come in, says when I make it to the concession stand. "What are we seeing today?"

One of my favorite things about The Reel—the boutique, Black owned, theater that plays a mix of old and new movies—is that they still do ticketed sales. I love the feeling of holding the paper in your hand, of having something tangible to remember the experience by. I don't know how or why, but it always makes it feel more real to me.

"The Sanaa Lathan double feature," I tell her, holding up the ticket as proof.

She nods her approval. "Love and Basketball and Brown Sugar, good choice. And what food items are we pairing our movies with?"

"My usual."

"Medium classic popcorn and a small coke," she recites, tapping the computer screen in front of her to ring me up.

"Classic is so boring," a soft, husky voice says from behind me. I turn in surprise, recognizing the sultry lilt before I even see Grayson's face. Her posture is relaxed, her heart-shaped face free of makeup and her curves hidden by the oversized, black hoodie she's wearing that's more for comfort than fashion. She's paired it with soft, black leggings and a pair of sneakers that effortlessly contribute to the monochromatic look I've come to expect from her.

Usually, I never feel weird about coming to the movies in my work clothes because no one but Jada is ever around to judge me, but standing in front of Grayson, who looks so casual and relaxed, makes me a bit self conscious because some sick part of me wants to look like I belong with her. Shaking that thought off, I search for a response that will strike the same playful chord her opener did.

I tilt my head to the side and give her a half smile. "I think you pronounced amazing wrong."

Her laugh is a soft sprinkle of warmth and humor that hits me right in the gut. "No, words like amazing are reserved for popcorn flavors like churro or truffle Parmesan."

"She's not wrong," Jada chirps.

I throw her a wounded look over my shoulder. "Oh, so you're just going to turn on me like that?"

Jada holds up both hands in mock surrender and takes a step back from the register. "Don't shoot. I mean, no shade to the classic, but the churro is superb. A fan favorite, if you will."

"Sure, but popcorn is supposed to be savory, not sweet."

"The churro is both," Grayson says, stepping up beside me so the smell of popcorn in my nostrils has now been replaced with the sweet, spicy notes of her perfume. Vanilla, lavender, ginger and coco. I turn the words over in my head again and again, using them to ground me and quell my reaction to her proximity. We haven't been this close in weeks, not since I toed the line of appropriateness when I touched her in the parking lot, and I don't quite know what to do with my hands because they want to touch her again.

This time just for the pleasure of it, not to protect but to feel, to explore.

Because that's completely appropriate.

Once again, I have to force myself out of my head and into reality where Grayson is now leaning on the counter, chatting with Jada like they're old friends. For all I know, they could be. It occurs to me then that I know nothing about Grayson outside her relationship with Brian and the few snippets of herself she's shared about her mom, aunts, and cousins. I don't know what she likes to do for fun or how she relaxes after a hard day. All I know are her hardships and ugly truths, and what I want is the quiet whisper of the things that bring her joy.

"Can I get a coke and a medium popcorn as well? Half churro, half truffle Parm," she says, reaching into her purse to dig out her card.

I place a staying hand over hers, putting an end to her search. "I got it."

"Oh, no, Xavier, I can't let you—" she protests, but it's too late because I've already tapped my card against the reader. Jada smirks as she leaves the counter to fix our orders, and we move over to the side to wait for them.

"Thank you."

"You're welcome." I pluck napkins from the holder in front of us, enough for two people with three different kinds of popcorn between us, and Grayson grabs straws for our drinks. It doesn't escape my notice that we came here separately but have both silently accepted that we'll be going through the rest of this experience together.

"Do you come here a lot?" I ask, immediately cringing at the way the question sounds like a cheesy pick up line.

The corners of Grayson's eyes crease, and she tries to fight it, but soon a laugh that's completely at my expense passes between her lips. I like her laugh. I like her laugh a lot.

"Yeah, I heard it as soon as it came out of my mouth," I tell her, chuckling along with her.

"*Come here often?*" She giggles at her awful attempt to emulate my voice, and I shake my head, enjoying seeing her this silly, this free.

"It was a genuine question."

"I know. I know. And I'm awful for laughing. I'm sorry."

"You know? I don't think you are."

She presses her lips together and pushes out several calming breaths through her nose. "Okay, okay. I'm done now."

I arch a brow. "You sure?"

She nods, wiping a tear from her eye before meeting my gaze. "Sorry. I really needed a laugh after therapy today."

The first time she mentioned she was seeing a therapist to me, there was a bit of shame wrapped around the letters of the word. It's not there today, though, and I'm glad about that, glad to know that she isn't judging herself for needing help to heal.

My shoulders rise and fall in a show of genuine nonchalance. "You don't have to apologize, Hart. I'm happy to be a source of amusement for you, especially after a grueling therapy session."

Something like confusion, and maybe genuine wonder, passes behind her eyes, and I can't tell if it's because of the way I've just used her last name or because of how mildly I've reacted to her laughing at me. After hearing all about how her future ex-husband had no problem making her the butt of his jokes but hated being the subject of hers, I know chances are it's the latter. I don't get to confirm whether my assumption is correct before Jada appears with our popcorn and drinks, though.

"Half churro, half truffle Parm," she announces, sliding the tub towards Grayson. "And a classic," she adds, aiming the second tub in my direction. Before Grayson can move, I scoop both of them up in my hands.

She gives me a playful roll of her eyes. "I guess I'll get the drinks."

"Enjoy, you two," Jada singsongs, skipping back over to the register after giving Grayson the drinks.

With our items in hand, Grayson and I leave the lobby and begin making our way down the short hallway to the left that houses the smaller showing rooms.

"You are seeing the double feature, right?" I ask, slowing my strides so she doesn't have to run to keep up with me. Grayson isn't a short woman, and her legs are model long, but they're still not as long as mine.

"Oh, yeah. I couldn't pass up a chance to see my two favorite Sanaa movies in one sitting. That woman is so fine."

"And has been fine my whole life," I add, stepping back as we approach the theater door so she can go in first because I don't want her to feel obligated to sit next to me. Apparently, like me, she's here to decompress and relax, and I don't want to impose.

"Right?! Every time I see her, she just looks better and better."

I hum my agreement, trying and failing not to notice the way her hips sway as she gracefully maneuvers up the stairs, climbing to the top row, which is where I prefer to sit.

"I always like to sit in the middle," Grayson explains, stopping right in the center of the row. She turns and looks up at me, auburn eyes bright and happy. "Is that okay with you?"

I should say no. I should hand over her popcorn, take my drink, and retreat to a different row, or maybe even a different theater, so that it doesn't feel like I'm on a date with a client, but I don't. I just stare at her for a moment, learning what joy looks like when it's etched into her perfect features, and then I nod.

"Yeah, that's good with me."

We share popcorn and laughs; I hold Grayson's hand when she gets emotional during the scene where Monica plays Quincy for his heart, and when both movies are over, and I know I should let her go, I ask her to share a meal with me. That's how we end up in a booth in the back of the small diner a few doors down from The Reel.

Grayson's knees bumping mine under the table.

My eyes trained on her face.

The food on my plate gone cold because I can't stop looking at her long enough to eat.

"Just admit it, you liked the churro popcorn," she teases, wiggling her brows at me.

"It was good," I concede. "But it's not better than the classic."

"Okay, now you're just flat out lying. Your hand was in my popcorn more than it was in yours."

She's not wrong. The cinnamon and sugar mixture on top of the already superior combination of butter and salt had caught me off guard. I tried it because she insisted, but I wasn't expecting to like it, to keep going back for more, to playfully fight Grayson off when her fingers intertwined with mine as we both vied for the same kernel.

I shrug. "I was just helping you out, since you had two different flavors to eat."

Her nose scrunches with disbelief. "You're a terrible liar, you know that?"

"Are you sure you don't want a box for you food, sweetheart?" Our waitress asks when she returns to the table with my card, two copies of the receipt and a pen.

I take everything from her and give her a smile. "Yes, ma'am, I'm sure. Thank you."

"He's all full off of churro popcorn," Grayson tells her, which makes me laugh. Our server clearly doesn't get the joke, and she gives us both a weird look as she walks away.

"Well, it's official. We can never show our faces here again," she murmurs, watching the older woman as she shuffles back to the kitchen.

Heaving a sigh, I purse my lips to feign disappointment as I sign the receipt. "Yeah, I think we'll probably have to take your stand-up act on the road. Surely, we'll find someone out there who understands jokes about varying popcorn flavors. We might need to tap into our connections in the movie theater circuit."

Grayson snorts a laugh and watches me rise from my side of the booth. When I'm on my feet, I offer her my hand, which she takes without a bit of hesitation, allowing me to hold on to her until we're out of the diner and back on the sidewalk.

"Where'd you park?" I look to the left and right, scanning the cars lining the road for any sign of her SUV and coming up empty.

She hooks a thumb over her shoulder, indicating the opposite direction from where I left my car. "A few blocks over."

"Alright, let's go."

Her lips part, everything about her expression saying she's about to say something like 'you don't have to do that,' but I shake my head. "Remember what I told you at the courthouse, Hart? No more treks to your car alone."

She tosses her head back and groans, spinning on her heel to face the direction we need to go. "Ugh, fine."

We fall into step, and I place my hands in my pockets while Grayson folds her arms against her body to brace herself against the chilly, February wind whipping around us.

"Mara texted to say you guys have filed the counterclaim," she says. "What happens next?"

The question about her case serves as a harsh, unwelcome reminder of the reality of who we are to each other. My reaction to it is so strong I almost give in to the urge to ask her if we can talk about this later, but I don't.

"Next, the judge will ask us to do mediation to see if things can be sorted outside of court."

"Brian won't go for that. Not after he reads the counterclaim."

"I know."

"So we'll have a failed mediation, and then what?"

I glance at her, studying the stoic lines of her profile. "Then we'll go to trial."

Grayson presses her lips together and nods slowly. I've noticed that's what she does when she's processing information. "And how long will that take?"

"There are a lot of factors at play when it comes to setting a trial date. The number of cases on the judge's docket. The temperature of his coffee the morning of the ask, whether he won his weekly poker game the night before. I'm hoping Bernard will throw some of his weight around and get the process expedited in an attempt to fuck with us."

As we approach her car, her steps slow, and she pulls out her keys. "Why would you want him to do that? Wouldn't it be better for us if we had more time?"

"Yeah, but it'll be better for you if you're free of him sooner rather than later."

It's a quiet, urgent confession that leaves me in a whisper and washes over Grayson in a soft wave. Several emotions skate across her features, and before I can catalog or name them, she's crashing into me. Her body soft and insistent as it sinks into mine. I wrap her in my arms, desperate to hold her, to grasp this fleeting moment that I know will end too soon.

"Thank you," she whispers, rising up on her tiptoes to press a gentle kiss to my cheek. I don't get the chance to respond, or react, because she's gone just as quickly as she came. I watch her rush to her car, missing the heat of her, wishing in that moment I'd been anything or anyone but her lawyer because then I could have kissed her back.

6

GRAYSON

"These look so good, Gray!" Kendra squeals, reaching out and squeezing my hand with one of hers while the other caresses the fabric of the pieces hanging on the clothing rack in my room.

She came over to drop Crew off with my mom and popped in to say a quick hello before she left to have yet another sit down meeting with his dad, Cash, about his inconsistent presence in their son's life.

This is probably the third come to Jesus meeting she's had with him in Crew's short life. He always promises to get it together, and for a while he does, but it's never long before things fall apart again. I know Kendra is tired of the back and forth, but she'll never give up, though, because she never wants Crew to say she didn't do everything she could to facilitate a relationship between him and his dad.

"Thank you! Do you think the cream will show as white in the photos?" I ask as she releases me. We both step back and take in the collection as a whole. The earthy color palette and the luxurious, yet accessible fabrics that are light and breathable, meant to be worn in the summer heat that will be upon us soon.

Originally, Kendra, Chantel and A'ja wanted me to try for an early spring launch, but I wanted to take more time to rebuild the brand and re-acclimate myself with Grayson Hart, the designer and CEO of Elysian. Some days, I still feel like an imposter, like I'm trying on someone else's skin, but most days, it feels right.

Today happens to be one of those days.

Kendra shakes her head, stepping forward to run her fingers over the cream drop waist maxi dress with a peplum hem. "I think it'll be fine. Amina knows what she's doing."

I nod, reassured by her confidence and the reminder of who will be behind the camera, capturing the pieces I've worked so hard to bring into the world. Amina Daniels, Jax's wife two times over, is a celebrated wedding photographer who has never had a single thing in front of her lens she couldn't capture beautifully.

"You're right. Mallory's gorgeous complexion will also lend the piece some warmth, keep it from coming across too white."

"Exactly," Kendra agrees, and we grin at each other. "You're really doing it, Gray. You brought your business back, rebuilt it from scratch and came back a million times better. I'm so fucking proud of you."

"Girl, why are you always trying to make me cry?!"

"Because it's nothing wrong with crying when they're happy tears," she says, bumping me with her hip. "I hate to make you emotional and run, but I have to go meet this man."

Her annoyance is evident in the wrinkles in her forehead and the narrowing of her eyes. I pull her into a tight hug and kiss her cheek.

"You're a great mama. You know that?"

"I do. I just wish I had done a better job of picking a daddy for my baby boy."

"There's always next time."

She breaks the hug with a small shove that makes me laugh. "Girl, I'm not having another baby no time soon."

"You don't have to have another baby to have another chance at picking a dad for your kid. Step fathers are a thing you know."

Scoffing, she turns towards the door, preparing to leave. I follow behind her, mostly to continue to get on her nerves, but also because I need to be heading out as well.

"I'm just saying, Ken," I continue, dogging her steps as she rushes down the hallway toward the front door. "A man doesn't have to be the father. He can be the father that stepped up."

She throws me a death glare over her shoulder but doesn't respond, refusing to play in to my shenanigans, choosing instead to address my mother and her son who are out in the backyard, barely visible through the glass sliding doors that lead to the patio.

"I'll be back soon, auntie. Crew, be good for Lottie Dottie!"

Neither of them respond. Not that she expected them to.

"I'm heading out too, ma!" I yell, grabbing my keys and purse from the table by the door. Kendra gives me an odd look as I follow her outside.

"Where are you going?"

"To meet Xavier."

My stomach does a little flip when I say his name, and I fold the smile that always wants to appear when I think of him between my lips. No one should like their divorce lawyer as much as I like Xavier. No one should like anyone as much as I like Xavier, especially not when they're coming out of a marriage as awful as mine and are just learning to really trust their judgment.

"Another movie date?" Kendra asks, her voice taking on that teasing lilt that it always has when she teases me about running into Xavier at The Reel months ago.

"No, we're prepping for trial." When my stomach flips this time, it's a result of the anxiety that courses through me every time I think about facing Brian in court. It's been a long time coming, and I'm more than ready to be done with all of this, but I still can't believe the day I've been waiting for since I left is finally here.

Well, almost.

The trial starts at nine o'clock tomorrow morning, and Xavier has spent the last few weeks drilling me, Kendra, Chantel, A'ja, Aunt Nita, Aunt Marcel and my mom with question after question about my relationship with Brian and the emotional abuse he subjected me to. I expected that I would have to testify, but I didn't really consider that everyone else in my family would have to as well. Thankfully, they were all more than happy to lend their voices to my cause and help make the case stronger.

According to Mara, we've all been ready to take the stand for days now, but Xavier, apparently, doesn't agree. He said that I've been a little shaky with my answers during cross and asked me to come in so we can go over them one last time.

"Oh." Kendra gives me a sympathetic pout. "Do you want me to cancel with Cash and come with you?"

I wave her off, knowing she would if I needed her to. "Absolutely not. I'll call you later, and we can exchange updates."

"Sounds good," she says, sending me off with a half-hearted salute. "Love you."

"Love you more. Good luck with Cash," I call out, climbing behind the wheel of my car and closing the door. I give her one last wave before backing out of the driveway and calling Xavier to let him know I'm on my way.

He answers on the first ring, his voice deep and rough. "Hart."

That stupid smile I fought back when I was in front of Kendra comes back in full force, pulling at the corners of my mouth and making me sound all silly when I attempt to mimic his serious tone.

"Allen."

He meets my terrible imitation with a soft, indulgent chuckle. "I assume you're on your way."

"Yep, I should be arriving at your office in twenty-ish minutes."

"Actually, there's been a change of plans."

"Oh." I pause, biting my lip. "Did you need to cancel?"

"Nah, nothing like that. I just want you to meet me at the court-house instead of at the office. Is that okay with you?"

I nod, even though he can't see me. "Yeah, that's fine. Pretty sure my arrival time will be the same."

"Alright, see you there."

"Okay. Goodbye, Allen."

Another light chuckle that makes my thighs clench fills the line.

"Bye, Hart."

When Xavier said he wanted me to meet him at the courthouse, I didn't really know what to expect, but it wasn't this. This, being me on the witness stand and him pacing in front of me with his tie hanging loosely around his neck and the sleeves of his crisp, white button down, rolled up to expose the veins in his forearms.

"Okay, Hart, final question."

He strides over and places both hands on the wooden rail in front of me. His stance is wide and imposing and his eyes are intentionally hard, meant to intimidate me.

"Ready?"

"Yeah, I'm ready."

We've been at this for hours, and I'm tired and hungry, plus I'm sure the bailiff Xavier bribed in order to get us through the door is fed up with sitting outside waiting for us to be done.

"According to your claim, there has been no point in your relationship with Mr. Lucas where he was not subjecting you to emotional or psychological abuse. If that's true, why did you stay with him for so long?"

I narrow my eyes at him, silently asking if he actually wants an answer because we both know for a fact that if this was the real deal, he'd object the moment Monty Barnes finished asking the question. Xavier dips his chin slightly, acknowledging the reason for my hesitation and asking me to continue, anyway.

"Because I loved him," I reply, my voice steady and sure. Pride shines in Xavier's eyes when I don't elaborate further. He's been on me to make my answers to questions like this concise, because it'll make it harder for the opposing side to use something I've said against me.

"Do you still love him?" he asks, his voice low as the words spill out into the space between us. The question catches me off guard, and I'm not sure if Xavier is asking as himself or if he's still pretending to be Brain's attorney, because this question has never been asked in any of our other prep meetings.

"I—"

"Concise answers, Hart," Xavier reminds me, leaning in even closer.

My breath stalls in my lungs, held hostage by the heavy weight of his stare, and yet, I find the strength to respond, knowing somehow that the answer needs to be spoken.

"No, I don't love Brian anymore." I study his face, watching for a reaction. He gives me nothing. "I'll always want what's best for him," I continue, still trying to read Xavier. "And I hope he wants what's best for me, too. I think we both know that's not him, though, that it probably never was him."

It's been months since I've cried over Brian and my failed marriage, so the tear that springs in my eye and rushes out over my cheek surprises me. What's more surprising, though, is the warmth of Xavier's palm against my jaw as he cups it, using the wide pad of his thumb to stop the tear in its track. For the second time tonight, I'm breathless, my chest burning, my lungs begging for air that won't come as long as Xavier Allen has his hands on me.

"Was that okay?" I ask, forcing the words out past the lump in my throat that just might be my pounding heart.

"It was perfect. You're perfect," he murmurs. His hand is moving now, his thumb going from my cheek to the corner of my mouth and then further to the left, until his tear stained skin is brushing over my lips, spreading the salted moisture over my flesh in a slow, deliberate stroke.

On instinct, I open for him, letting his finger slip past the barrier of my teeth and into the warm recess of my mouth. He hisses out a curse as I suck the last remnants of my emotional release from his skin, and I moan around the intrusion. My eyes are glued to his face, watching wonder and desire crash together to make some new, unnamed emotion that holds Xavier hostage as he pulls his thumb out and pushes it back in, fucking my mouth with one hand while the other wanders over the barrier between us and walks an incendiary trail up my parted thighs.

It's been warm lately, April bringing us rain and the first whispers of heat, so I'm wearing a dress. When I put it on, I thought it was simple and unassuming, with a hem short enough to show off my legs but long enough to be considered decent, but now, with Xavier's large hand disappearing beneath it, it feels explicit. Like I only designed it to obscure my vision as my divorce lawyer's fingertips graze my pussy lips while I'm sitting on a witness stand.

Xavier's eyes meet mine. "Can I?" he asks, the words coming out as a rough groan. With his thumb still fucking my mouth, the only thing I can do is nod and open my legs wider, silently begging him to do whatever he wants with me.

We're together in this madness. I can feel it in Xavier's touch. I can see it in his eyes. Whatever line we're crossing here, we're dancing over it together, and I'm ready. Xavier is too. He's right here with me. His fingertips grazing the edge of my underwear. His pupils dilating with anticipation. My chest heaving and my pussy throbbing as he lifts the lace from my skin, and then…the door opens.

"You two almost done here?" the bailiff, whose name I didn't catch, asks, bursting into the room. His sudden appearance shatters the moment, and Xavier pulls away. His finger leaving my mouth with a wet smack while agony and regret write themselves into the lines of his face.

He grips the wooden rail again, knuckles turning pale from the force of it, and glances back at the bailiff. The moment is already broken. I know that, but I'm still disappointed when Xavier says yes, when the door closes and the bailiff is gone and instead of putting his hands back on me, he goes over to the table and begins to gather his things.

I stand on wobbly knees and step down from the witness stand, exhilarated and embarrassed all at once. Did I really just suck that man's thumb? The question bounces around my skull as I grab my purse and start for the door, intent on leaving Xavier and whatever spell he placed me under behind.

"Where are you going, Hart?"

His voice is a lot closer than I thought it would be, telling me he's no longer at the table but, instead, just a few paces behind me. My steps falter, but I don't turn to face him. I can't.

"Home. You said we were done."

"And we are, but you're not leaving without me walking you to your car." He places his hand at the small of my back, urging me forward. I don't know what else to do, so I move, passing through the door of the courtroom when Xavier holds it open for me and letting him guide me out of the empty courthouse, into the parking lot and to my car in complete silence.

I almost let us leave it that way, with the moment on the witness stand lingering between us, but I know I won't be able to sleep tonight if I don't get some clarity on the situation. Xavier is clear across the parking lot when I find my voice, but he stops when I call out to him, turning back around slowly in order to face me.

"For the record," I say, my voice echoing between us. "Back there on the witness stand, that moment, you did want—"

I stop short, unsure what noun to pair with the exemplar of desire.

It?

Me?

Neither feel exactly right. Thankfully, Xavier doesn't need me to elaborate. He nods, and when he speaks, his words strike a chord in my heart that's linked directly to my sex.

"More than I've ever wanted anything."

7

GRAYSON

Three Months Later

"**I** do. I did. I'm done," I read the words out loud while the bass of the song A'ja just requested the DJ play thumps in my chest.

The letters of my supposed divorce mantra glows in the light of the lit candles lining the exterior of the cake Chantel sat in front of me, and although it's stupid, and a little too Pinterest circa 2010 for my taste, I can't help but smile.

I am done.

After months spent in the presence of the relentless force that is Xavier Allen and countless hours rebuilding my life and business, I am done.

Divorced.

Free.

And not quite as broken as I thought I'd be when the ink dried. That's not to say the process wasn't hard. That there weren't moments when I thought it'd be easier to walk away with nothing than continue to fight the legal machine that is the Lucas family. That there weren't times, like the day of trial when Brian and Noelle walked into court holding hands, when I wondered if there was no end to the embarrassment and shame of having once loved that man. But there was an end, and this is it. I'm living in it.

"Say it like you mean it, hoe," Kendra shouts, holding up a glass of champagne. "You said you do. You did. And now you done!"

A laugh bubbles past my lips, infectious in its nature as it passes to every one of the women in the booth around me. It's only the four of us —me, Kendra, A'ja and Chantel—but we're loud enough to be a group double our size. Even Chantel has come out of her shell, drinking and squealing and cracking jokes with the rest of us. This little divorce party was actually her idea. She said one of her co-workers did it when she split with her husband last year. The older lady had opted to stay at home and burn her wedding dress after she trashed it with her friends, but A'ja talked us into putting our own spin on it, which is how we've ended up bouncing from one club to another over the course of my first Saturday night as an officially single woman.

Luxe, the newest club leaving its mark on Fairview's nightlife, is our fourth and final stop. Kendra suggested we save it for last because she claims they have the best selection of men to end your night with. I told her I wasn't planning on taking a man home tonight, but it didn't stop her from forcing me into every piece of sheer, lace or skin tight black fabric in my closet until we landed on an outfit everyone but I agreed was my look for the night.

Personally, I thought the strapless, black corset made of nothing but mesh and satin covered boning that hugs my ribs and accentuates my curves while exposing my stomach and almost all of my breasts was a bit too much for a night out on the town, but then Kendra talked me into pairing it with black, wide leg cargo pants and black heels with a pointed toe and suddenly the look came together. It's the perfect mix of casual drama and glamorous nonchalance, which is exactly what the vibe at Luxe is.

"Come on, Gray." Chantel nudges me, her eyes wide, encouraging and maybe a bit mischievous. It's that bit of mischief that gets me to comply. I pick up my glass of champagne and lift it to meet Kendra's, and everybody follows suit. They're as quiet as they've been all night as they wait for my declaration, so I decide to just go for it.

"I DO. I DID. *I'M DONE, BITCHES!*" I scream before tossing back my champagne and gulping the bubbly liquid down in one go. The women around me cheer and whoop their approval, turning my mantra into their own so that I'm blowing out the candles on my divorce cake to a chorus of: *"She said she do. She did. And now she done!"*

"Y'all weren't half as enthusiastic at my wedding," I muse once the cake is cut and we're all eating the small slices of chocolate goodness we took before the server assigned to our table spirited it away and replaced it with more alcohol.

"That's because nobody wanted you to marry his ass," A'ja retorts, tossing her blonde, knotless braids over one slender shoulder.

"I know, A'ja," I sigh, hoping conceding that fact will stop her from going off on her 'Brian was never any good' tangent. They've become more frequent now that Brian and Noelle are openly together. "But I'm saying, it was a party with free food, free drinks. Bernard even paid for everybody's flights to the Bahamas. Even though I was marrying the wrong man, y'all should have still had a good time."

Lord knows I didn't. Brian and I spent the entire week arguing about everything from the time of the ceremony to the fact that his mother insisted on having two outfit changes during my day, and both of the dresses were white.

"*I* had a great time," Kendra chimes in.

Chantel rolls her eyes. "Girl, we know. You came back pregnant with Crew."

Kendra smiles fondly at the mention of the snaggle tooth, almost seven year old who has us all wrapped around his finger. When Kendra found out she was pregnant, we were all shocked because she was only twenty-one and hadn't yet graduated from college, but we still rallied around her. Mama, Aunt Nita and Aunt Marcel took turns staying with her during the week, cooking and cleaning and taking care of things so she could focus on school and being a mom.

A'ja, Chantel and I stepped in where our mothers couldn't and Crew's father wouldn't, which means we all got to play integral roles in his life. Even now, with her career well under way and her confidence in her abilities as a mother through the roof, not much has changed. We're still the village Kendra leans on, and she's still our resident hot girl with looks and sass to match her big ass brain.

"You right, you right," she replies, giggling into her hand. "Cash was slinging that vacation dick, and your girl had to catch it."

"He needs to start slinging some child support your way," A'ja says, rolling her eyes.

Kendra, like me, is used to her little sister's comments, so she just laughs and picks up her ever full glass of champagne and takes a sip. "Girl, you ain't never lied."

"Speaking of cutting checks," Chantel says, shifting in her seat to pin wide brown eyes on me. "When do you get your divorce settlement?"

My stomach flips at the thought of the eight-figure amount Xavier secured for me. It's twice the amount I'd planned to walk away with, and I nearly fell out when the judge announced that he'd be awarding me the money from the trust created per the terms of my post-nup AND requiring Brian to match the amount.

Biting my lip, I split a smile between my three cousins. "It cleared this morning."

It's loud in the club. Like really loud. But the moment the women gathered around me process my words, they explode into maniacal cackles and ear-splitting screams that draw the attention of everyone around us.

Heat creeps into my cheeks, and I shake my head. "Y'all are ridiculous."

"No. What's ridiculous is me paying for bottle service when you got millions sitting in your bank account," A'ja says with wide eyes.

"You cursed me out and said my money was no good here when I offered to pay," I remind her.

"That was before we knew you could have bought the entire club out."

I wrinkle my nose at Kendra's statement. "Why would I buy the entire club out? Then it would just be the four of us and that wouldn't be any fun."

"True," she agrees. "And tonight is all about fun, which means…"

"Uh oh," Chantel says under her breath, suspicion taking over her features as she takes in Kendra's wiggling brows and bouncing shoulders. "You know what she's about to say, right?"

"I know, and it's only a matter of time before A'ja joins in," I whisper, matching her suspicion and faux dread with the ease that's existed between us for our entire lives. As sisters who are only two years apart, Kendra and A'ja have always had the other to play off of, but Chantel and I are both only children, so we have an unspoken agreement to join forces in the face of their chaotic sibling bond.

As expected, A'ja takes one look at her sister and immediately shifts into party mode, pushing to her feet and nudging her sister out of their side of the booth. "It's time to dance," she says, finishing the sentence Kendra started.

Chantel and I don't bother protesting because we know it's useless. After all, the whole point of tonight is to look good, have fun, and be seen. All three goals are easily within reach as soon as we take up space in the center of the dance floor, reciting lyrics about wet ass pussies at the top of our lungs while we make sure that any man who approaches one of us doesn't overstay his welcome.

We're six songs in when my throat gets dry, so I catch Chantel's eye and hook a thumb over my shoulder to let her know I'm going to the bar. She waves me off, too caught up in grinding on the man who has her waist in a death grip to give me a verbal response, and I laugh to myself about just how far my uptight cousin has let her hair down as I weave through the dense crowd and secure what looks like the last open spot at the bar.

"A water, please. Keep the change," I say quickly, catching the attention of the lone bartender—a visibly stressed Black girl with ginger faux locs—before she moves to the other end of the bar where multiple people are waving her down. She takes the twenty I slide her and tucks it into the front pocket of her apron before retrieving the bottle and handing it to me. I crack the top and offer her a smile, hoping the bit of kindness will make her day a little better. "Thanks."

"You're welcome," she calls out over her shoulder, leaving me to hydrate while she goes to handle the rowdy customers waiting for her.

"Sure you don't want something stronger?" Someone asks from behind me just as I'm swallowing my first sip. I turn slowly, following the dark, velvet notes of a voice I've grown accustomed to over the last six months, giving myself time to absorb the reality of hearing it pitched low with the intention of melting away inhibitions and stealing common sense, to wonder if this is how he always sounds when his gravelly timbre isn't stained with professionalism.

Even though I'd already identified him by his voice alone, I'm still surprised when Xavier and I come face to face. It's been a while since I've seen him in person. After the trial, most of our communication has gone through Mara or happened over email. I haven't allowed myself to think too much about why that might be.

He runs a large hand over those waves, genuine shock in low, hooded eyes as he takes me in. Suddenly, I'm entirely too aware of the amount of skin I'm showing, and I have to fight the urge to cover myself, to hide from the dark eyes roving over my frame, lingering a little longer on the space where I know, despite every single one of my cousins telling me otherwise, my bare nipples are peeking through.

He clears his throat and brings his gaze back to mine. "Grayson"

"Xavier."

"What are you doing here?"

"Oh, you know, just celebrating my divorce."

"Right." He nods, and a smug, prideful grin tugs at the corners of his mouth, calling my attention to his full lips and the perfect lines of the dark beard and mustache surrounding them. "Congratulations, again. You deserve every cent you got from that bastard."

"Thank you." I bite my lip to stave off the surge of emotion that rushes through me unexpectedly. "Not just for the congratulations, but for everything you did to make it necessary. I wouldn't have gotten through this without you."

He waves me off, which is exactly what he did the last time I thanked him for keeping every promise he made to me during our first meeting. "You don't have to thank me, Hart. I was just doing my job."

My cheeks heat in the stupid way they always do when he makes my last name sound like a term of endearment, and I take another sip of my water before responding. "Well, you're damn good at it."

"That's what they tell me."

We share a short laugh over his lack of humility before silence stretches between us. I wrack my brain for something else to say but come up empty. I don't know how to do this with him, how to act now that we're no longer client and lawyer. I assumed he wouldn't know how to do it either, but he looks so at ease.

He tucks his hands into the pockets of his jeans. "So, I'm sure you're glad to finally be done with lawyers."

"Only the ones with the last name Lucas."

"Oh." He takes a step towards me, towering over me even though I'm easily six feet tall in these heels. "Does that mean I get to stick around?"

My shoulders rise and fall in a casual shrug that suggests it doesn't matter to me one way or the other, that I haven't been thinking about that night on the witness stand for months. "If you want," I say, turning back to the bar and taking another sip of water because being subjected to the intensity of his gaze when I'm also a little tipsy is making my knees feel weak.

Clearly, he does want to stick around. He steps up to the bar too, taking up space beside me. It's a tight fit, so he has to angle his body to make it work, which means half of his six-foot-five inch frame is pressed against my side and all the air around me is now laced with the notes of sage and cedarwood that make up his scent.

"You here alone?" he asks, lips so close to my ear the question steals my breath away.

Shaking my head, I turn to him, bringing us face to face. "That'd be a sad divorce celebration, wouldn't it?"

Xavier lifts his hand, signaling for the bartender, while his eyes stay on me. When I was his client, I never allowed myself to be moved by the butterflies that would take flight in my stomach every time he held me hostage in a discerning stare. I told myself that my over reaction to prolonged eye contact was just a sad indicator of how severely disconnected Brian and I were from each other.

Tonight, I tell myself that all of those things might be true, but it doesn't change the fact that I like how this man looks at me. That I'm pleasantly surprised by the fact that someone who charges hundreds of dollars an hour for his time doesn't reserve his rapt attention for clients. That even now, when I'm no longer paying him for his attention, he's still a study in active listening and thoughtful responses.

"I guess that depends on if this is the true celebration or a prelude to the real thing," he answers finally, and I find myself unable to speak for a moment because I'm trying to sus out whether he meant for his words to be laced with innuendo. I'm certain it's deliberate. Xavier is always so careful with his words, always aware of the thousand different ways people can read into the things he says.

More than I've ever wanted anything.

His words from that night echo in my mind, and I push them away, knowing what they do to me. The way they make me long for things I've spent months convincing myself he doesn't want to give.

"What do you mean?"

"I mean some divorce celebrations end when you leave the club, and others—" he licks his lips, and my stomach twists into a knot when dark brown eyes with specks of gold sprinkled in the irises ghost over the lines of my corset accentuating my cleavage before working their way back up to my face, "—others start at the club and end in somebody's bed."

My core clenches at the thought of ending up in his bed, and I'm breathless when I respond. "And I'd need to be here alone for it to end that way?"

"Are you here alone, Grayson?" he asks again, reminding me I never actually answered him the first time.

I bite my lip. "No, my cousins are here with me."

I swear I see disappointment skate across his features, but if it was there, it's gone by the time he speaks again. "I'm surprised you guys talked Chantel into coming to the club," he says, craning his neck to see where the bartender is. I peek over the bar to get a look too and see the same girl from before slowly making her way back down to us.

"I think she's the only one working, so it's going to take her a while," I tell him. He sighs and drops his arm, resting his elbow on the lacquered wood.

"Are you here by yourself?" I ask, eyeing the bills in his hand that look like more than enough to cover a few rounds of drinks.

"No, my brothers and best friend forced me to come out," he sighs, trying to sound put out even though he's fighting back a smile. "They claim I work too hard and don't make any time to celebrate my wins." He tips his head to the side, pinning me with an imploring gaze. "Does that sound like me?"

"It does actually."

Truthfully, I don't know much about Xavier Allen, but I do know that he's a classic workaholic. His entire life is his clients, his cases and his firm, which can't leave time for much of anything else. After how hard he worked on my case, I'm glad he's out celebrating a hard earned win.

"Wait." I hold my hand up, interrupting whatever response he was about to give me. "What other cases have you closed lately?"

His brows furrow. "I've had a few custody cases settled in mediation, but the most significant case I've closed this week is…"

"Mine," I finish for him. "So, you're here celebrating my divorce, too."

8

XAVIER

I thought I had this woman all figured out.

Since the day she hired me, I've spent every billable hour, and a few free ones too, learning every part of her, digging into the most intimate parts of her life, studying what she looks like when she's holding back tears or curbing the burning desire to murder someone, mastering the art of delivering the perfect motivational speech to get her to channel that energy into something other than a destructive act that would hurt her in court.

By the time I prepared the final order of divorce, I felt confident that my knowledge of my client, Grayson Hart, was vast and incredibly detailed. I can say with the same amount of confidence that I don't know a damn thing about the woman sitting next to me right now. The woman who heard I was celebrating her divorce and, instead of getting upset and calling me a crass asshole, which I would have deserved, invited me, my brothers, Lincoln and Chance, and my best friend, Orion, to join her and her cousins.

Our two parties meshed easily, turning into one big 'Grayson is finally free' celebration where conversation and drinks have flowed easily but done nothing to distract me from the waves of shock that wash over me every time I look at her.

She's traded in the reserved, slicked back bun she usually favors for wild, tousled curls that linger around the soft lines of her bare shoulders before cascading down her back. For as long as I've known her, she's always gone for a more natural look with her makeup, but tonight her plump lips are painted maroon and those wide, auburn eyes have been lined and purposefully smudged for a dramatic, smoky effect.

The true departure, though, is the outfit she's wearing. The black on black ensemble looks amazing against her mocha skin. I've seen her do the monochromatic thing a million times before, but never like this. Never in something as revealing as the corset she's wearing tonight. My eyes fall shut of their own volition, and I curse silently as the image of her at the bar flashes in my mind once again.

The fucking corset.

Most men can't tell the difference between one that was made to look like lingerie but is actually meant to be worn outside of the bedroom, and one that was made for the bedroom and found its way outside, but I can. And the one Grayson is wearing is meant to be worn for five seconds before being wrenched from her curves and resigned to the floor of someone's bedroom while the skin it was just covering is caressed and kissed and worshiped.

"You okay?" A soft, yet husky voice asks through pillow soft lips that graze the shell of my ear. The music is loud, so it stands to reason that her proximity is more of a necessity than a desire for closeness, but I still react to it, to her. Three months of waiting for the right time, the right moment to cross the line we started dancing around on that witness stand have left me raw, an open nerve that her voice grates over in the most deliciously, painful way.

Opening my eyes, I turn to find that she has moved closer to me. We're alone in the booth now. Everyone else in our combined party has paired off and taken to the dance floor. I'm surprised by how enthusiastically my brothers and Orion have taken to her cousins, but I guess I shouldn't be, since I know firsthand how intoxicating the women in this family can be. I've been intrigued by Grayson from the moment she walked into my office, and the more I've gotten to know her, the less that's changed.

"Yeah, I'm good," I tell her, taking a sip of my bourbon, hoping the familiar burn will knock some sense into me. "I was just—"

"Falling asleep in the club?" she asks, her lips curved into a teasing smirk that pulls a laugh out of me.

"Nah, just trying to remember if I signed off on a brief before I left for the day."

"So, thinking about work at the club?" She twists her lips to the side. "That might be worse."

"Worse than falling asleep? I don't think so."

"No, I think it is. You can't help it if you doze off for a second, but thinking that hard about work is intentional."

"I wasn't thinking hard."

"Your face was scrunched up, your brows were pulled together. That's what you look like when you're thinking hard."

Her voice is full of authority, and I'm more pleased than I should be at the thought of her knowing me. I throw back the rest of my bourbon before I reply. "I guess you're right, but it's an important brief."

Why I'm choosing to continue with the lie instead of changing the subject altogether is beyond me. I guess I like how Grayson's eyes are dancing with amusement, how her posture is relaxed and engaged, how she's leaning forward, all of her attention on me.

"I'm sure it is, but you're supposed to be celebrating, sir, not thinking about work."

My mind wants to linger on the shape of her lips when she calls me sir, but I force myself to move past it. "You're supposed to be celebrating too," I remind her.

"I've been celebrating all night," she shoots back, her voice laced with pride as she kicks out her legs to show off the heels on her feet. "Me and these bad boys have crossed the threshold of every club in Fairview."

"Did they make it to the dance floor, though? Or did you just go from the door to a private section?"

A small wrinkle born of light-hearted offense forms between her brows as she leans in close to me. Her breath is a ghost of warmth on my lips, tinged with the flavor of champagne. "You think I'd wear heels I couldn't dance in all night to my divorce celebration?"

We're already too close, but I lean in too, eating up the small bit of distance between her face and mine. "It's a fair question, no? I haven't seen you out there—" I jut my chin toward the dance floor and the dense crowd enjoying the mix the DJ is spinning, "—since I joined your celebration."

"That's because someone needed to keep you company while you sat here and thought about work."

"And that someone just had to be you?"

"Well, yeah, because it wasn't going to be any of them," she insists, glancing towards the center of the floor where her cousins and my crew have been for the past twenty minutes. They've paired off. Lincoln with Chantel, Chance with A'ja, and Orion with Kendra, the two of them dancing too slowly for the song that's playing.

"You're right." My eyes drop to her mouth to watch the slow spread of the smile she always gives me when I agree with her. The way she reacts, and my knowledge of the asshole of a man, makes me think she rarely heard those words from her husband. Ex-husband, I remind myself. Grayson isn't married anymore. I dedicated a lot of my time and energy to make sure that became an undeniable truth.

"Of course I am," Grayson says, pulling away from me so she can finish the glass of champagne she's been nursing for a while now. When the flute is empty, she places it on the table and pushes it towards the center before rising to her feet. "Are you done thinking? Because I want to dance."

A bright bubble of surprise blooms in my chest. *"With me?"*

She tilts her head to the side. "Well, yeah, unless you don't want —" she pauses, a flicker of uncertainty flashing behind her eyes that makes me feel like a dick immediately. I've let uncertainty fester for too long between us, and I'm determined to use tonight to kill it, to show her I meant what I said in the parking lot of the courthouse all those months ago.

"No!" The word tumbles out roughly as I rush to stand. Grayson steps back, still unsure. I reach for her, catching her by the wrist and dipping my head to meet her eyes. "I mean, yes, I'd love to dance with you, Hart."

Almost instantly, the doubt that was just marring her features melts away, replaced by a brilliant smile that sends warmth spreading through my chest and down my spine. My grip loosens on her wrist, fingers trailing down the soft skin layered over her pulse, which jumps at the contact. I link our hands together, and Grayson gives my fingers a light squeeze as I lead her to the dance floor, intentionally avoiding my crew and her cousins because I don't want to share the moment we're about to have with anyone else.

As soon as we're settled between the shoulders and bodies of strangers who instinctively make room without us having to ask, the music changes to something slow, sensual and full of bass. I turn to Grayson to find her biting her lip. This isn't the dance she had in mind.

"Do you—I mean we could—" I tip my head back in the direction we just came, letting her know there won't be any hard feelings if she's rethinking this.

"No, I'm good. Unless you—"

I cut her sentence short with a tug on her hand that brings her chest to mine and place both hands on the generous span of her hips. "This okay?"

"Mhmm, almost," she hums, spinning around to press her back to my front. Then her head tips back, coming to rest on my shoulder, and she starts to move. Beginning with a slow roll of her hips that makes me curse under my breath and wonder how the fuck I'm going to keep my shit together for the length of the song.

With my gaze cast heavenward and a prayer that I don't end up fucking this woman in the middle of the dance floor on my lips, I follow Grayson's lead. Every twist, sway and roll of her body is a guide that I follow with the dedicated interest of a student at the feet of their teacher, eager to please, desperate not to do anything that might make this already surreal experience end before I can fully appreciate the heat of her body pressed against mine.

"I should have known," she says, flicking those auburn eyes up at me.

"Known what?" My lips are at her ear. My fingers digging into her waist. My chest is pressed to her back, and there's no space between us. No line to look at and tell us how far past appropriate we've gone.

"That you'd be a good dancer." She turns in my arms, and now we're face to face. There's more space between us now, more breathing room, but somehow, with her arms on my shoulders and her fingers linked at the base of my neck, this feels even more intimate. "You're good at everything you do," she whispers, eyes locked on mine as she delivers the compliment. In any other context, it might feel innocent, and maybe she means it that way, but that's not how I take it. And how can I when she's this close, and she smells this good, and her body is all curves and movement and sin?

"I'm just following your lead."

"You're good at that too, so I guess my point still stands."

"It does," I concede easily, my voice a rough edge of a waning control that fades a little more every time Grayson's hips roll into mine. She's still looking at me. Her gaze low, pupils blown, teeth dug into the plump flesh of her bottom lip as I match her move for move. Our bodies locked in the pale imitation of an act I've been desperate to perform with her since I became acquainted with the slick, wet heat of her mouth.

As if she knows I'm thinking of her mouth, Grayson leans in close and brushes her lips over mine. The action is so gentle, so subtle it can't even be called a kiss, but it still hits me deep in my chest, sending sparks of electricity down my spine and straight to my dick.

"*Hart.*" My voice is strangled with surprise and desire as I follow her retreating lips, desperate to keep them close.

"Touch me," she says, the demand dragging me further away from the line I've never even been tempted to cross with another client.

"Where?" I ask, my hands already moving, already exploring as images of the last time she granted me permission to touch her flash through my mind.

"Everywhere."

Grayson spins around again, leaving her right arm over my shoulder so that her body is one long line of displayed temptation. A canvas I've been given permission to paint with curious, unhurried hands. Before I start my quest, I pull her hips back into me, letting her feel exactly what her proximity has done to me, and a quiet moan leaves her lips at the feel of my erection pressed into her ass. An answering moan is pulled from my chest when she starts to grind against it.

"Fuck, Grayson."

"Touch me, Xavier," she whines. Leaving one hand on her waist, I drag the other up her body, fingers splayed wide over her rib cage and the satin lines of the corset hiding her skin from me, and wonder if I've ever heard a sound sweeter than Grayson Hart begging. As I cup her full breast in my palm, thumb grazing over her nipple, I decide I haven't.

I also decide that I want to hear it again.

That I want her begging for more while I have my tongue buried in her pussy and the insides of her thighs are already slick with her release.

That I want her pleading to sit on my dick and bounce those perfect titties in my face.

That I want her whines of desperation to echo off the ridiculously high ceilings of my bedroom.

And now that I've decided, now that I've accepted we're well and truly past the point of appropriate interaction between a lawyer and his client, former or otherwise, I know I have to have it.

I have to have *her*.

Grayson's eyes are closed now, but they pop open when I go from rubbing her nipple to rolling it between my thumb and forefinger, and they stretch wide with surprise and need when I say, "Come home with me."

9

GRAYSON

Brian is the only man I've ever slept with.

Our sexual relationship started long before he ever thought to claim me publicly. I was tutoring him in algebra. He and Noelle were on a break, and it just kind of happened. And it kept happening, never turning into the outward facing affection and intimacy I craved until our sophomore year of college when Noelle cheated on him and he came crawling back to me, claiming he wanted something more.

The sex we had that day was amazing, probably our best work to date, but I already know it won't hold a candle to what's about to happen between Xavier and I. The energy between us is different. The way he touches me and looks at me and talks to me is different. Everything he does oozes passion and power and control. Nothing like the refined disinterest Brian would give me no matter what I was wearing or doing.

"Stop thinking about him," Xavier growls into my mouth, following my naked form down onto the plush, dark comforter covering his king size bed.

"I wasn't—"

"You were, and I get it, but you're with me right now, Hart, so *be here* with me," he says, shifting all of his weight to his hands so he's hovering above me.

There's no anger or annoyance in his eyes, only understanding that stems from his knowledge of my history. I start to question the wisdom of this, of making the first man I've slept with since my divorce the man I had to lay my soul bare to over the course of months, but before I can decide if I should try to change my mind, Xavier comes down, pressing the hard planes of his bare chest into my breasts and kissing me.

His kiss is firm, but his lips are plush perfection, and his tongue. My God, his tongue is a weapon he's far too adept at deploying. He strokes it in and out of my mouth, coaxing moans from me that he laps up with earnest while his hips rock into my core. His hardened length gliding through the slickness coating my pussy lips.

"C—condom?" I gasp, pulling back to break the kiss.

Xavier's pupils are blown, his eyes two black holes of desire that threaten to swallow me whole. No one has ever looked at me like he's looking at me right now, and I don't know what to do with that information or the rush of warmth it sends through me, trickling down from my pounding heart to my throbbing sex.

He comes back down for another kiss, this one shorter but no less intoxicating before lifting off of me completely. "We're not there yet, Hart," he chuckles, sliding down the bed until his head is between my thighs. "I haven't even tasted you."

My eyes go wide with surprise and a little fear as he takes my thighs in his hands and places my legs on his broad shoulders. "Oh, no, you don't have to do that," I gasp, trying to close them.

Both of his brows fall together in a line of confusion. "You don't want me to?"

"No. I mean, I don't know—I've never. No one's ever—" Heat floods my cheeks, and I throw my head back on the bed, wondering how the hell I thought I could sleep with this man when I can't even tell him I've never been eaten out before.

"Never?" Xavier asks, incredulity threaded through the warm breath passing over my skin. There's still no judgment in his tone, but there's no understanding this time, either. When I gather the courage to lift up and look down at him, he looks genuinely confused. *"Never, Hart?"*

I answer his question with a quick shake of my head, and his fingers flex against the outside of my thighs as my head hits the mattress again, questions about the likelihood of dying of embarrassment bouncing around my skull.

"Because you didn't want to or because he didn't?"

Squeezing my eyes shut, I force my breathing to even out. "He didn't. He always said it was… *gross*."

He also always gave me the most disgusted looks when I would ask for it in the early months of our sexual relationship. Eventually, it got to the point where I felt disgusted with myself for wanting it. I don't tell Xavier that, though.

"What a fucking loser," he groans the words into my skin, his head rocking from side to side like he's physically pained at the idea. "You were wasted on him."

I don't respond. I don't think I can respond because I'm too focused on the heat from his mouth on my overly sensitive skin and the growing wetness pooling in places I'm sure he can see.

"Grayson," he murmurs, the syllables of my name stretched and torn over the sharp edge of desire. "You're getting wetter."

"I know."

"Let me taste you, Hart. I promise you'll enjoy it."

The confidence in his tone, coupled with his concern about my pleasure, is almost enough to make me scream yes, but I manage to hold it in, knowing I need one more thing before I give in to him.

"Will you?"

"It's mostly about your pleasure, but, yeah, Hart, I'll enjoy it. If I'm being honest, I'll probably enjoy it a little too much. You might have to pry my mouth off of this pretty ass pussy because once I experience you coming apart on my tongue, I'm going to want to make it happen again." He nuzzles against the inside of my thigh, the hairs of his beard tickling my flesh and making me squirm. "And again." He nips at my mound, then plants a soft kiss over the freshly abused spot. "And again." He nudges my clit with his nose, sending a jolt of pleasure through me.

My entire body is burning with anticipation, alive with the desire to have the experience Xavier is promising, so neither of us is surprised when my lips part and a breathless, "Yes," slips past them.

Xavier wastes no time. As soon as I give my consent, his head dips down, and he's French kissing my pussy. His moans of satisfaction vibrating against my clit, radiating through my body as I arch up and grab hold of his head with both hands, the tips of my nails disappearing into the thick, black waves hugging his scalp.

"Fuck, Xavier."

I feel rather than see his answering smile. It grows bigger when he lowers my hips back to the bed and brings his hands to my core, making them complicit in his bid to devour me. He holds me open with his left, two fingers parting my lips to expose my most intimate parts to him, and drives into me with a finger on the right. It's the most exquisite intrusion. I rock into the shallow thrusts, silently urging him to give me more, screaming my overwhelming pleasure when he obeys, adding another thick finger to the mix while his tongue assaults my clit with long, laving licks that are precise and messy all at once.

His timing is perfect. His touch awe-inspiring. He doesn't need any help from me, but I still find myself holding his head in place, unable to let go for fear that he might change something and cause the pressure building inside of me to retreat. And I can't lose it. Not when it's this strong and coming on this fast, not when it's the first orgasm I've had in almost two years that wasn't a result of my own efforts, not when it's Xavier giving it to me.

More than I've ever wanted anything.

That's what he'd said to me that night, and if I didn't believe him then, I damn sure believe him now because *this*? <u>This </u>is how you eat a meal you've been desperate to have for longer than you'd care to admit.

It's that thought that sends me careening over the edge of control and into a pool of pleasure I'm content to drown in. True to his word, Xavier keeps his mouth on me long after I've come back up for air. He suckles on my clit, raw, reverent groans of pleasure pouring from his throat as he coats his mustache, his lips, and his beard in my essence.

"No more," I whimper, feeling the beginnings of a second orgasm unfurling low in my belly. It's not that I don't want to come again, I just don't want to come without him. I want him inside of me, his weight pressing me into the mattress, his lips at my ear while he talks me through it.

The entire bottom half of his face is glistening when he finally pulls back, a proud smile curving those sinful lips. He climbs up the bed, covering my body with his, and kisses me long and hard.

"*Now*, I can get the condom," he says, arching his body over mine to reach the nightstand to his right. While he's digging through the top drawer, I busy myself with tracing his sides with my hands and laying a kiss on the side of his pectoral. It's a stupid, intimate gesture that has no real place in a one-night stand but feels right between us. Xavier seems to agree, the evidence of his approval shining in his eyes when he's back between my legs, resting his weight on the back of his heels as he makes quick work of putting on the condom.

Then he's back on me, gentle hands shifting wild curls out of my face as he studies me. "You okay?"

I lift my legs and clamp them at his sides, linking my ankles behind his back to keep him close. "Perfect."

"That you are," he says, reaching down to align himself with my entrance.

The first inch of him is enough to let me know I'm going to be sore for days after this. The stretch is almost painful, almost too much, but it's so good I don't dare ask him to stop.

"More?" Xavier asks, planting a kiss at the corner of my mouth. I turn my head, catching his lips in a slow, nasty kiss laced with my scent and taste while my hips rock up, taking him deeper. Now it's his turn to curse and moan and beg, and he does all of those things with his mouth still attached to mine, all of it a silent inference I make while his dick slips further and further into my soaked channel until he reaches the end of me.

And then we curse together, we moan together, we beg each other for relief and release and something we can't put words to but is satisfied by the wet glide of Xavier's dick retreating from my walls and pushing back in.

"Jesus, Hart," he rests his forehead against mine. "You're gripping my shit so tight."

Panic rises in me. That old fear of being wrong twisting my stomach. "Sorry, I didn't…"

He rears back and drives into me again, turning my apology into a helpless moan. "Don't you dare apologize, Grayson," he growls into my ear. "This pussy is perfect. *You're perfect.*"

And just like that, the panic is gone. Melting into the back of my mind as pleasure arrives at the forefront. Its presence inspired by Xavier's mouth at my neck, kissing, sucking, and biting while he drills into me over and over and over again, fucking me up the bed and, when my head hits the headboard, flipping me over.

His hands go to my waist, pulling me back onto his dick. "Look at that fucking arch," he moans, fingers digging into my hips as I start to move, taking over the rhythm to keep him where I need him while pleasure from his praise makes me wetter.

Xavier comes down, partially covering my back with his front and laying reverent kisses along my spine as his hands move from my waist to my breasts, fingers toying with my nipples and heightening the sensations that are already rolling through me.

Needing more, I rise up on my knees, forcing Xavier back so we're both kneeling. His teeth find the lobe of my ear, and his every breath harsh, heavy pants that challenge me to drive down harder, faster, taking him deeper with every fierce stroke while moans pour from my lips.

"Give it up, Hart," he whispers, meeting me thrust for sinful thrust while my walls tremble around him. "I can feel it coming," he says, one hand leaving my breasts to apply pressure to my lower belly, making everything more intense.

One of my arms goes up, looping around his neck. "*Xavier.*"

I can't keep the rhythm, can't speak a word that's not his name, can't do anything but feel the weight of his hand on my stomach and the strength of his presence at my back and obey the simple command that he keeps repeating while every part of him works to help me do so.

"I want it, Grayson," he says, using his knees to spread me out further. His other hand abandons my breast, skating over my ribs to make a home between my thighs where he pets my clit with soft strokes of his fingers that make my eyes roll into the back of my head. "I want it more than I've ever wanted anything."

And it's those words that do it.

That cause me to fall apart around him, that triggers the unholy echoes of staggered orgasms that leave us both shattered, and one of us wondering what the fuck she's done.

* * *

"WHAT DO YOU MEAN YOU LEFT?!" Kendra whisper-shouts, her face wrinkled in disapproval and confusion while A'ja, Chantel and Amina all give me variations of the same expression.

We're sitting in the middle of Refrain, the restaurant Jax and Amina opened in New Haven, a small city about forty-five minutes from Fairview, a few years ago. The space is big and bright and warm, a far cry from the cold, modern look of his first restaurant, Arcane, which was the brainchild of Jax's failed home-wrecker of an investor, Cassidy Marks. When the realtor, Luca Adler, first brought me to this spot, I knew it'd be perfect for the communal eating, farm-to-table vibe Jax wanted to go for. I also knew the large, open space at the back of the building would be great for hosting events.

I didn't, however, know that one of those events would be a fashion show to re-launch Elysian. For months, this brand and my divorce have been my sole focus. Now, the divorce is done, and the launch is a few weeks away, and suddenly, everyone wants to hear me talk about other things in the middle of what's supposed to be brunch with a side of business.

Personally, I blame Amina for asking how my divorce celebration went. Her inquiry led to everyone pressing me for information about Xavier and what we did after we left Luxe. Unfortunately for me, the strong ass mimosas Jax keeps sending to the table gave me loose lips, and I ended up spilling my guts about my night with my divorce lawyer, sparing no detail. Not even the one about tip-toeing out of his apartment in the wee hours of the morning after falling asleep in his arms.

"Why would you leave, Grayson?" Amina asks, copper eyes filled with confusion as she hands a crayon to Maya, the beautiful, almost two-year-old she and Jax conceived not long after their reconciliation.

"Gwayson no leave, Mama," Maya exclaims, pointing a finger sticky with syrup in my direction. "Gwayson, right there."

Kendra throws her head back and groans. "She's too cute, Amina. My ovaries can't take it."

"Yes, they can," A'ja retorts, rolling her eyes. "You already have your hands full with Crew."

"I mean, I know that, but look at her, A'ja! Look at those cheeks." Kendra reaches over and pinches Maya's cheeks, making her giggle. All of us swoon, even A'ja and Chantel, who, as far as I know, have no interest in being mothers.

Pride shines in Amina's eyes as she looks at her daughter. "Thanks. I made her from scratch."

"Umm, excuse me, you had some help," Jax says, sauntering up to the table with a dish of something delicious smelling in his hand. He sets it down in the middle of us and scoops Maya up out of the booth, raining kisses down on her face while she giggles and tries to hold him off with two tiny hands on either side of his face. Jax makes a big show of acting like she's actually holding him back, chomping at the air between their nearly identical faces.

Amina watches them, and there's love evident in her expression even as she waves them off. "Help me out right now and take her in the kitchen with you so I can have some adult conversation."

Jax honors her request with a dramatic dip of head and a faux curtsy. "As you wish, my liege." We all wave goodbye to him and Maya as they make their exit, her happy giggles lingering in the air long after they're gone.

"Okay," Amina says, clasping her hands together and sitting up straight to indicate how serious she is. "Now, tell me, why did you leave?"

Stalling, I lean forward and grab the serving spoon from the dish Jax just brought out. "I wonder what this is," I muse aloud, and they all groan. Chantel snatches the spoon from my hand, doling out a hefty helping of the food onto everyone's plate.

"It's a Spanish omelet, Gray. Now, tell us why you left that man's bed," she orders.

From the moment the conversation shifted to Xavier, I've been trying, and failing, to fend off thoughts of last night. The way he touched me, the way he fucked me, the way he held me until we both fell asleep. The way his brow furrowed when I slipped out of his arms, like even in his sleep, he could sense that I was gone.

"Because," I offer lamely.

Unsurprisingly, no one at the table appreciates that answer, and they stare holes into the side of my face while I push eggs, potato and chorizo around on my plate. Not bothering to eat any of it.

"Because what?" Amina asks, eyes wide with recognition, with knowledge of what someone looks like when they're running away from something, or rather someone, they should be running toward.

I sigh and drop my fork, pushing my plate away. "Because I didn't want to spend my first night as a single woman in anyone else's bed but mine. I got divorced to regain my independence, not give it away to the first man to show interest in me after Brian."

Never in my life have I seen so many sets of eyes roll at once.

"Grayson." Chantel puts a hand on my arm, her tone soft. "I mean this in the most disrespectful way possible. That's some bullshit."

My mouth drops. Chantel hardly ever uses curse words, so for her to just be casually dropping them in the middle of this awkward, but lighthearted, conversation has surprised the hell out of me.

"It's not!" I protest, looking around the table to find support and coming up empty.

"It is," A'ja says. "You're talking like spending the night was going to result in him putting a ring on your finger or something. There is a such thing as casual, extremely gratifying sexual relationship with no strings attached."

"This is true." Kendra picks up her glass and holds it in A'ja's direction, proposing a toast. "I fuck Cash every now and again when my other dudes ain't acting right."

A'ja, who was just preparing to reciprocate the act of camaraderie, frowns at her sister and sets her glass back down, silently gagging. "You need to stop that immediately."

Amina and Chantel laugh as the two sisters start to argue, both of them tossing out things that the other should stop doing. I tune them out, thankful that the conversation has shifted so I can be alone with my thoughts. Immediately, they wander to Xavier, to what it might look like to have something with him that won't require me to offer parts of myself I'm not quite ready to give, parts that came rushing to the surface when I was in his bed last night.

Now that the option has been brought to my attention, I know that it's something I want. Something that feels safe for me. Something that would allow me to have more of what we shared last night, but at no risk to myself.

The only question is: would Xavier want that with me?

10

XAVIER

I want whatever pieces of Grayson Hart she's willing to give me.

I knew that was true the first time I met her and proved it to be fact when I let her believe she was escaping my bed unnoticed almost a week ago. I'd felt her absence the moment she decided to leave, her mental detachment from what we'd just shared stealing her away from me before she even moved a muscle. Letting her go was hard but necessary. After years of only sharing her body and heart with one man, I knew she'd need time and space to process being with someone else. I didn't like having to give her either of those things, but I sucked it up because she's already spent too much of her life putting someone else's needs before her own.

"You're going to be late," Mara says, poking her head through the door and interrupting my thoughts. She tilts her head to one side, wide eyes assessing me. "What's the matter?"

"Nothing."

My quick response only makes her more curious, and instead of closing my office door and continuing on her journey out of the office to begin her weekend, she steps inside. I let out a long sigh, not in the mood to deal with an inquisition. Mara doesn't care. She plops down in one of the armchairs across from me and narrows her eyes.

"Tell me the truth."

Hoping to move this conversation along quickly, I start to clear off my desk, stuffing papers into files and separating them into piles that indicate their varying priority levels. Mara waits patiently for me to finish, then arches a brow at me. "Are you done procrastinating?"

"I'm not procrastinating," I say, rising from my desk and putting the few files I need to take home with me in my briefcase. "I'm just waiting for you to realize that whatever is on my mind is none of your business."

"So there *is* something on your mind."

"I'm a lawyer, Mara. There's always something on my mind."

The snaps from my briefcase sound off, punctuating my statement. Mara rolls her eyes and pushes to her feet, falling into step beside me as I make my way out of the office. "Personal or professional?"

"None of your business, Mara," I insist, even as flashes of Grayson beneath me fill my head, the sound of her moans playing in my mind like my favorite song on repeat.

She nods, using my deflection as confirmation. "So, personal then."

We step onto the elevator, and I remain quiet, scrolling through the group chat I have with Orion, Lincoln, and Chase. They're unusually active today, most of the messages in the thread related to the logistics of the grand opening of Orion's restaurant and lounge, Pulse, which is happening tonight. Even though Orion is my best friend, my brothers, Lincoln and Chase both jumped at the opportunity to invest in his business with me. Together, we purchased the building that used to house Arcane, the restaurant Grayson's boss, Jaxon Daniels, used to own. It shut down not long after his departure, leaving the building and all the equipment to sit for months with no interest or offers until we came along, getting it at a steal.

"Is it Grayson?"

I cut an eye at her, trying to sus out how much Mara knows. She's not a lawyer yet, but she already knows and lives by the first rule of practicing law: never ask a question you don't already know the answer to.

Pocketing my phone, I cross my arms and meet her gaze straight on. "How did you know?"

A shit-eating grin pulls up the corners of her lips as she pumps a celebratory fist. "Yes! It's about time you admitted it."

"I haven't admitted anything."

"Not verbally, no, but your face says it all," she says, pointing an accusatory finger in my direction.

"Pure conjecture." I shrug, annoyed at how easily she reads me. "With no evidence to back it up, your argument is dead in the water."

"Okay." Mara turns to face me, squaring her shoulders as she prepares to deliver the facts of the case. "The following facts are not in dispute: one, you represented Grayson in her divorce and went harder for her than I've ever seen you go for any other client." I start to argue, but she waves me off. "Two, you billed her for half the hours you worked and refused to invoice her even after she got that big ass settlement. Three, Grayson ended her divorce celebration at Luxe, which is exactly where you went on that same night. It stands to reason that you two would have run into each other and maybe even acted on the feelings you've been trying to hide since that cute little movie date y'all had back in February."

The elevator comes to a stop, depositing us on the parking level reserved for our firm's employees. Mara's parked a little further down than I am, so we bypass my car to get to hers first.

"How do you know where her celebration ended?"

"Because she invited me. I got a whole itinerary from her cousin, Chantel."

"Why didn't you go?"

She fishes her keys out of her purse, tapping one button to unlock the car. "Because I didn't think it was appropriate to be partying with clients, but now that I know you slept with her, I'm thinking that might have been fine." My jaw drops, and Mara bursts out laughing. "Oh, my God! I was totally bullshitting, but you actually slept with her?"

Once I pick my jaw up off the floor, I level her with a stare that has her turning serious. "Do you think that's a good idea?" she asks.

I run a hand over my hair, hating how closely Mara's question resembles the one I've been asking myself since Grayson walked out on me. Technically, there are no rules prohibiting me from pursuing a romantic relationship with a former client. I mean, it's not exactly encouraged, but it's common enough in my field that it won't have me appearing before any ethics boards.

My true concern isn't the potential professional ramifications, it's the personal ones, more so for Grayson than for me. She has no experience dating, and I've been playing the field for as long as she's been tethered to Brian's useless ass. Which isn't to say that I'm some expert on romantic endeavors because I'm not. My last serious relationship was years ago, and it faded off rather than ended because I checked out and she forced herself not to care anymore, so my nonchalance hurt less.

Long story short, Grayson and I were both woefully unprepared for us. For the way it felt to be together like that. Our souls lain bare, rubbed raw, ripped apart and put back together, fused in some way that feels irreversible.

"I don't know," I admit quietly, wishing I could be more certain, wishing I knew more than the fact that it just feels right to be with her, and not just when she's underneath me or on top of me or in front of me, her back arched and her legs parted to give me room to slide into her from the side. Clearing my throat to expel the wayward direction of my thoughts, I give Mara a thin smile. "See you Monday."

She sends me off with a wave of her hand and no words of encouragement, which I strangely appreciate. When I'm thinking about how to come at a problem, I don't like having other people's voices floating around in my head, their opinions keeping me from forming my own. By the time I arrive at Pulse, I've decided that I have to approach this shift in my dynamic with Grayson the same way I approached our first dance: by following her lead. I trust her to tell me what she wants, to communicate her needs and limitations, and I hope that she'll trust me to do the same.

"X, man, it's about damn time you got here," Lincoln, my baby brother, says by way of greeting when I arrive at the table Orion reserved for us. He stands to pull me into a one-armed hug, followed in close succession by Chase, who claps me on the shoulder with those big ass hands he got from our dad.

"What's up, bro?" he says, letting me go and sinking back down into the booth, long arms hanging over the sides.

I return their greetings and glance around the dark, moody space that's filled with people, but not the person I'm looking for. "Where's Ma?"

My mother, Dahlia, was supposed to ride to the opening with me, but she decided I was taking too long and opted for a ride with my brothers instead. I expected to find her at the table with them, but I should have known she'd be somewhere working the room, teaming up with Orion's mom, Liz, to find all the eligible ladies to set one, or all, of us up with.

Lincoln shrugs. "Somewhere around here."

"I think I saw her at the bar," Chase offers, scanning the room to confirm his theory. When he spots her, he nods. "She's right there in the middle, talking somebody's head off."

Following his gaze, I find our mother through the crowd. Her short, platinum blonde hair styled in the finger waves she's been rocking since the 90's and the large gold hoops she won't let go of make her hard to miss, but it's the person she's sitting next to that draws all of my attention. Even though I can only see the side of her face, I know her immediately, and I start moving in her direction without a second thought. When I get close enough to inhale the warm notes of her perfume, both she and my mother turn to face me.

"Hi, my baby!" Ma smiles brightly, the bangles on her arm clinking together softly as she opens her arms for a hug that I give her while my eyes linger on Grayson's face.

"Hey, Ma."

"Grayson, this is the son I was just telling you about." She leans back, holding me at arm's length and gazing at me with proud eyes. "My oldest, Xavier. He went to law school, graduated top of his class, is the youngest named partner in his firm, and…" Her voice trails off, and she looks between Grayson and I, eyes wide with surprise when she sees the way we're staring at each other. "And you two already know each other," she finishes, slipping off the barstool next to Grayson to stand beside me.

"Hey, Hart."

Grayson's eyes turn molten, and I know that if the melanin in her skin would allow for it, I'd see the red from a growing blush tinting her cheeks. She takes a slow sip of her drink and licks her lips, making me remember what it's like to kiss her.

"Hi," she murmurs, refusing to call me by my first or last name. That bothers me. I want my name on her lips the way they were the other night. I want the syllables wrapped around her tongue, desperate and clinging as she falls apart beneath my touch. My inappropriate thoughts must show on my face because Ma slips away suddenly and quietly, leaving us to sit in the heavy weight of too many things left unsaid.

I take the seat next to Grayson. "What are you doing here?"

A smirk forms on her lips as she tilts her head to the side. "Are you going to ask me that question every time you see me out in the wild?"

I huff out a laugh. "No, this is the last time I promise."

"Kendra asked me to come with her," she says, shaking her head at me, still smiling. "Orion invited her."

"Really?"

"Yep. Apparently, they exchanged numbers at Luxe and have been talking every day."

Between the revelation that my best friend has been in regular contact with her cousin and the mention of the night I've been obsessing over for days, I'm at a loss for words. Grayson finds that funny.

"I don't think I've ever seen you not have anything to say."

"It doesn't happen often," I admit just as the bartender walks up to take my order. "Two fingers of the Balblair single malt and another one of what she's having." I slide a few folded hundreds in their direction and instruct them to keep the change before turning my attention back to Grayson.

She's wearing black again tonight. A color I've come to associate with her smooth, mocha skin and the generous dips and curves that make up her body. On anyone else, an all black ensemble might come across as somber, but on her—especially in the clearly custom made mini dress with the hem riding up her thighs—it gives regal, sensual, *fuckable*.

As if she can sense my thoughts, Grayson looks away, scanning the length of the bar, probably looking for Kendra so she can walk out on me again. Studying the soft lines of her profile because she won't give me her eyes, I wrack my brain for something to say to bring her attention back to me.

"So, you met my mother."

Now, she turns her head and her gaze snags on mine. "She's lovely, and she's very proud of you. She told me you went into family law because of her."

My brows rise, and I cast a furtive glance over my shoulder even though I know Ma won't be anywhere to be found. I want to ask her how, and why, that conversation came up with someone who is a complete stranger to her. She usually doesn't include the details of the emotional and psychological abuse my father subjected her to that resulted in a break from reality that landed her in a mental health hospital and Lincoln, Chase and I in a foster home in any of her "my son is a lawyer," speeches.

"Oh, yeah? How'd that come up?"

"She watched me turn down several very handsome, very charming men and asked me what the hell was wrong with me." Grayson chuckles, the warm sound hitting me like a swift kick to the ribs. "I told her I'd just gotten divorced and was over men at the moment. That resonated with her, and we just kind of ended up trading horror stories. She told me I shouldn't let Brian make me give up on finding love and that finding your stepfather healed something inside of her, and then she asked me if I wanted to meet her oldest son."

There's a dull ache in my chest that's existed right beneath my sternum since I was a kid, that came roaring back to life when I met Grayson and saw that distant look in her eye. I recognized it instantly, having seen it in my mother's for so long, and I'm happy as hell that neither of them have it anymore, that I was able to contribute to Grayson's liberation in a way I was too young to do for my mother.

"Did she at least do a good job of selling me?" I ask, voice rough with unchecked emotion.

Grayson nods, but she doesn't laugh at my attempt at lightheartedness. "It was a great pitch. I can tell she's been working on it for years."

"Decades, really. She's desperate for some grandkids."

"Ugh." Grayson rolls her eyes, taking another sip of her drink. "Aren't they all? You should hear my mama and aunts when we're all together. It's all they talk about these days."

"Doesn't one of your aunts already have a grand kid, though? Crew, right? Kendra's son?"

"Yeah," she whispers, her eyes shining with appreciation at my superior recollection. "He's about to turn seven, and we all adore him, but apparently he's too old to meet their grand baby requirements. I think the final straw was him suddenly deciding he was done with stuffed animals and giving away his whole collection."

I twist my lips to the side, considering her theory. "Sounds plausible. There's a definite correlation between a kid making developmental strides and the desire for a new baby. I'm pretty sure my mom got pregnant with Chase the same night I decided I no longer needed to sleep in her bed."

"I doubt that was intentional. She probably just got caught up in the thrill of being able to bust it wide open without a kid in the room."

My nose wrinkles in disgust at her phrasing, and she snorts out a laugh. "Oh, grow up, Allen. You and your brothers are living, breathing proof that your mom got it in at least three times in her life."

Disgust rolls through me again, this time manifesting in a full body shudder that has Grayson doubled over, clutching her sides. "You're gross," I tell her, smiling at her amusement despite being sick to my stomach at the topic.

"And you're childish," she tosses back. "Everyone has sex, Xavier. Including your mom."

"I mean, I know that, but I don't want to think about it."

"Well, duh. No one wants to think about anyone having sex, especially not their mothers."

The bartender reappears, sliding our drinks in front of us before disappearing again. I grab mine, taking a long sip of the brown liquid, letting the smoky flavor fill my lungs.

"Not true," I say after swallowing. "There are plenty of people I'd happily think about having sex."

Grayson arches a brow. "Like who?"

I don't even have to think about my response. It flows past my lips in a smooth wave laced with desire and whiskey. "You and me, for starters."

Her teeth sink into her bottom lip, and she shakes her head. "Walked right into that one, didn't I?"

"You did. I didn't have to take the bait, though. I'm sorry."

"Don't be. I figured we'd have to talk about it at some point."

"Not if you don't want to," I assure her, hoping like hell she does want to.

She shifts in her seat, angling those mile long legs in my direction. "I shouldn't have walked out like that."

"Grayson, you don't owe me any explanations. You did what you felt was best for you at the moment, and I respect that."

Auburn eyes race over my features, trying to find out whether I actually mean what I say. She must find what she's looking for because her features soften, vulnerability writing itself into the lines of her expression. "Is that why you didn't call?"

"Well, yeah. I was trying to give you the space you so clearly needed." Now, I'm searching her face, wanting to know what's going on in her head. "Did you want me to call?"

"Yeah," she breathes. "I wanted you to call."

There's easily a hundred people in this room. Music playing, drinks flowing, conversations happening all around us, but right now, there's just Grayson. There's just us. There's just her soft confession, and my hands that long for her skin and refuse to be denied the right to touch her any longer. I reach out, fingers hesitant as they wrap around the supple flesh covering her calf, growing bolder and more familiar when she doesn't pull away. Grayson gasps when they run a short circuit up to her knee and down to her ankle. I only get to do it twice more before she covers my hand with hers, a warning shimmering in her irises.

"What else?" I ask.

Her brow furrows. "What?"

"What else do you want, Hart? From this? From me? I'll give you whatever, do whatever, *be* whatever you want me to be. I'll take whatever pieces of yourself you have available to give as long as I get to have some of you." She shakes her head in disbelief and overwhelm, and I use my free hand to grip her chin, forcing her to focus on me and not the doubts swimming in her mind. "I know you have limits and demands, Grayson. I want to hear them all. I'm going to meet them all, so don't be afraid to speak them. Not with me."

It takes her a while. Long, agonizing seconds where the music feels too loud and everyone feels too close, the pitch of their voices too sharp, threatening to pierce the bubble around Grayson and I. By some small miracle, it doesn't break.

"I can't do serious," she says, her jaw turning rigid underneath my touch. "After Brian and the divorce, I'm just not ready for anything like that."

"So, you need casual. Understood."

"No, not casual. Just un-serious."

My lips quirk as I fight the urge to tell her that those words mean the same thing. She sees me biting the reminder back, and she smiles too. For a minute, we stay like that, smiling at each other over some unspoken thing. Finally, I respond, dipping my chin in acknowledgment of her amendment to my statement.

"Un-serious," I repeat, leaning in to close the distance between her face and mine. Her breath skates over my lips. "That's what you want us to be, Hart?"

"Yeah, Allen. Is that what you want?"

"More than I've ever wanted anything," I murmur before finally taking her lips in a kiss that's desperate enough to make us forget the lie we've just told ourselves and each other.

11

GRAYSON

"Fuck buddies?"

I grimace at the phrase, hating it all the more because it's on my mother's lips. To her credit, she looks horrified to be repeating them. A fact I would feel bad about if I hadn't just caught her eavesdropping on the conversation I started having with Kendra that now, apparently, includes everyone—models, hairdressers, make-up artists, Amina and the photographers and videographers she brought on to help capture Elysian's relaunch.

This day has been in the works for months, and even though I know I've done everything I can to make it perfect, my stomach is still in knots, my brain racing through a to-do list that's a million miles long. With only thirty minutes until the fashion show is slated to begin, and a large portion of the brand's hundreds of thousands of fans already logged into the live stream on Instagram, I should be doing something, anything, besides explaining my situation with Xavier to a room full of people that includes my mother.

Narrowing my eyes at Kendra, who started this line of conversation, I turn to find Mom waiting patiently for my explanation. "No, Mom. Xavier and I are not fuck buddies." Kendra and A'ja snort, and I glare at them over my shoulder, shifting to address them and everyone else in the room, acutely aware of the way Mallory is smirking at me as she rubs a shimmery body oil into her arms.

"We're just two adults who care for each other and have extremely gratifying sex every now and again." A shiver runs down my spine at the thought of all the ways Xavier and I indulged in each other last night at my new place. He ate my pussy on the stairs, then fucked me on the floor in front of my bedroom door before urging me into the shower, where he took me against the wall and put the stamina of my water heater to shame. I'd had to put him out after that, knowing if he stayed the night I'd risk showing up here late and disheveled but well fucked.

"Sounds like fuck buddies to me," Mom insists, breaking into my thoughts.

"I don't know," Mallory says, pushing to her feet and striding over. I've only known her for a few months, but it's safe to say I'm obsessed with the mahogany skinned goddess. She's all fire and sass and unrefined power. Plus, her body is incredible.

At our first fitting for the dress she's modeling tonight, I told her I wanted to design an entire line of pieces based on her proportions alone. Her husband, Chris, had hummed his approval, offering to pay me handsomely for the line and throw in a bonus if at least one of the pieces had a tear away component. Mallory giggled at the request, laughing harder when I started to blush.

She comes to a stop beside me, an easy smile on her lips as she integrates herself into our small circle. "Fuck buddies sounds kind of harsh to me. Maybe friends with benefits is a more accurate description."

I nod while Chantel shakes her head, her eyes on the clipboard in her hands, but her attention on the conversation. "Call it whatever you want. Any word that isn't 'relationship' is wrong."

My stomach flips, and I put both hands on my hips, shoulders high and tense with defensiveness. "Xavier and I aren't in a relationship."

No one seems to believe me. I'm not even sure I believe myself, but I have to stand my ground because giving even an inch right now would mean facing truths I've resigned myself to keeping buried in the recesses of my mind.

"Are you sleeping with anyone else?" A'ja asks, moving over to Mallory to fix a wayward strand in the cloud of curls on top of her head.

I press my lips together, fiddling with the pincushion in my hands, and Mom laughs, reading my expression accurately. "We'll take that as a no."

"It doesn't mean anything, though! I just haven't met anyone else I would want to…"

Kendra silences me with a wave of her hand. "Is Xavier sleeping with anyone else?"

"No."

I didn't ask for the information— because un-serious and exclusive don't really go hand in hand—but Xavier had volunteered it. In that moment, and still today, I refused to acknowledge how happy that made me.

"And is he showing up to other women's fashion shows completely uninvited, with a big ass bouquet in hand?"

Chantel's question has all of our attention shifting to her and then following her gaze to the open doorway where Xavier is indeed standing with a large bouquet of red roses in hand. I drag my gaze up his frame and all the way back down, noting how delicious he looks in the black on black ensemble and gold jewelry that makes him look like he's supposed to be standing next to me all night. He moves through the room with a singular focus, all of his attention on me even though there are a million different things happening around him.

I love when he looks at me like that, like nothing and no one else exists for him. My heart squeezes at the thought, and I force it away, knowing that if I'm not careful, I'll get used to that look, that I'll come to depend on it, that I'll start to want it to only belong to me.

By the time Xavier reaches me, everyone has found something to do that makes them look busy but keeps them within earshot. As she walks away, I hear Mallory mutter something under her breath about getting rid of Chris if divorce attorneys look that good, which means my lips are curved into a smile that's part disbelief— because I know she's never going to leave her husband— and part possessive pride because of the compliment.

"Happy to see me, Hart?" Xavier asks, leaning in close and dropping a kiss on my lips. It's chaste and familiar, sweet like the scent wafting up from the flowers in his hands.

"Always," I murmur against his lips, a little too much truth in the statement.

Xavier arches a brow as he pulls away. "Careful, I might start to think you actually want me around."

"Are these for me?" I run a finger over the petals of the roses, ignoring his statement because it's too close to the truth, which is that I'd regretted my decision not to tell him about the launch as soon as I got here to today.

Something about seeing Jax here supporting Amina, and Chris here supporting Mallory, made me long for Xavier. For his smart mouth and assessing eyes, for his small gestures of support and sneaky little ways of boosting my confidence. There was a part of me—the one that runs parallel to the part of me that decided not to invite him because I wanted to prove I could do this without a man—that wanted to call him and ask him to come, but I'd refrained, knowing I'd feel worse if I reached out and he denied me his presence.

He takes a step back, holding the bouquet out of my reach. "That depends."

"On?"

"On whether I can stay," he says, voice soft but rough. "I mean, I'll probably give them to you either way, but in case you need an extra incentive." The smile he gives me is lopsided and a bit self-deprecating, like he hates himself for asking because he might be crossing a boundary, and it warms my heart, but not as much as what he says next. "I promise I won't get in your way. I just want to be here to share this moment with you. You've worked so hard for this, and I want to cheer you on in person, not on a live with a million other strangers on the internet."

A wave of emotion crests inside of me, crashing into a rolling body of warm, liquid happiness that crowds my vision for a moment. Lifting up on my tip toes, I wrap my arms around Xavier's neck and squeeze him tight. He's momentarily stunned at the sudden show of affection, but it doesn't take him long to reciprocate. The petals of the flowers brush against the skin bared by the backless dress I'm wearing, and he kisses my cheek.

"Stay, please," I whisper in his ear before retreating from his embrace, conscious of all the eyes on us, even though they're not on Xavier's radar at all. His attention is only on me. His smile wide and lined with satisfaction as he holds the bouquet out for me to take.

"These are yours."

Taking the flowers from his outstretched hands, I bring them up to my nose and inhale deeply, trying to remember the last time Brian bought me flowers and coming up empty. Realizations like this used to hurt, used to press salt into the open wounds my marriage left me with, but now it doesn't move me at all. It's just a simple fact that I get to set aside along with all the other baggage I used to carry.

Brian never bought me flowers, but Xavier does, and if ever I want some when he doesn't feel the need to provide them, I can buy them my damn self. That's the power of this moment in my life. The gift of having someone who does nice things for me, being able to do them for myself as well, and knowing that in both instances, I deserve them.

I deserve nice things.

The thought echoes in my mind. And after the show begins, when I'm watching my dreams come to fruition from the wings with Xavier at my side—his hand resting on the small of my back, his thoughts and praises for every piece in my ear—it occurs to me that out of all the indulgences I've allowed myself to have since leaving Brian, this thing with Xavier might be the nicest of them all.

After the show is done, we move from the event space to the dining area of the restaurant to gorge ourselves on all the deliciousness Jax and his team have put together for us. He refused to let me pay for anything, saying it was the least he could do after everything I've done for him and his business over the years. As far as parting gifts go, a free catered dinner from a renowned chef for a party with over a hundred and fifty people in attendance is a damn good one.

"What's going on in that head of yours?" Xavier asks, laying a kiss on my shoulder while gazing up at me with heated eyes. If we weren't sharing a table with my family, I'd probably tell him that the moment he spoke all of my thoughts shifted to sex, but since we're far from alone, I go for a more tame answer.

"Just thinking about how good life is right now."

His fingers, which have never been resting on my thigh, run a smooth, soothing line over the fabric covering my skin, and I shiver. "How good you've made it."

"Hmm?" My breath stalls in my lungs, making me acutely aware of the liquid heat pooling in my core as he comes ridiculously close to my pussy and then retreats.

"How good you've made it," Xavier repeats, his voice pitched low. "All of this goodness is your own doing. A result of your strength, your courage, your resilience. Don't use passive language to make it seem like it just happened. *You* made your life good. *Say it.*"

Up until this very moment, I had been cataloging all the good things in my life. Holding them close so I could access them whenever I needed to be reminded that I was no longer the woman Brian half loved and gleefully abused. But never once did I acknowledge myself as the source of those good things, as the catalyst that created the conditions in which they were born, but right here, right now, with Xavier's eyes on my face and his hands on my body, and his words ringing in my ears, it's kind of impossible not to see it that way, to not want to speak it.

I lick my lips, tasting the unspoken truth on my tongue. "I made my life good."

The kiss he gives me afterwards catches me off guard. His mouth crashing into mine before I've gotten the words out completely. Despite how quickly it comes on, the kiss is relatively tame, lasting for long, devastating seconds filled with just the right amount of tongue before we come up for air.

"Well, now I've officially lost my appetite," A'ja says, glaring at us from across the table as she pushes her plate away.

Xavier chuckles, the humor filled sound low and dark as it curls around me. "Sorry, A'ja."

She doesn't respond, her attention now on the tablet in her hand that she's been using to monitor sales on the website. Her mouth is hanging open, and her eyes are wide. "Holy shit. We sold out!"

"What?!" I yell, standing up just enough to reach over the table and grab the tablet from her hands before sinking back down into my seat, eyes glued to the screen. My heart pounds against my ribcage as I take it all in. The bright red letters under every piece in the collection spelling out the words 'out of stock.'

I turn to Xavier, hands shaking, tears blurring my vision, and shove the tablet into his hands. "Tell me this is real."

He glances at the screen even though he already knows. After one cursory sweep over the screen, those dark eyes find mine. He reaches up and grips my cheek. "It's real, Hart, and it's everything you deserve."

12

XAVIER

For as long as I can remember, I've always thought of my mom as some superhuman entity. I guess it came from years of watching her survive, watching her endure, watching her constantly pick herself up and find the strength to be a good, loving mother to us. Even when we were no longer in her care, and she couldn't sort the truth of her dedication to us from the lies and poison my father had filled her with, she was still all of those things to me.

In my close to forty-years of living, I've never seen her bested by anything, but the flu she's fighting right now is damn sure coming close. She called me a yesterday, already horribly congested and running a fever that had her bordering on delirium, asking me to bring her some medicine and the grocery items she needed to make her famous chicken noodle soup. Being the obedient son that I am, I promised to bring her everything she asked for if she agreed to let Lou, my stepfather and her husband of fourteen years, make the soup. She agreed, but once I got over here with all the necessities in hand, she let it slip that Lou was traveling for work and wouldn't be back until next week.

Which is how I wound up spending my Thursday night in her

kitchen, stirring chicken noodle soup with one hand and checking my phone for a response to a text I sent hours ago with the other.

"It's a lot easier to cook when you use both hands," Ma muses from her perch in the living room. She's nestled in one of the recliners Lou loves, a blanket wrapped around her and a face mask covering her mouth to protect me from her germs. Typically, she likes to curl up on the chaise attached to the large sectional. If I had to guess, I'd say today's change in seating preferences is because of the way the recliners line up perfectly with the opening between the living room and the kitchen, allowing her to watch my every movement without having to stand.

Laughing, I turn the temperature on the eye down and place a lid on the pot. "All the cooking is done. Now, we just have to let it simmer so the flavors can marry."

She pulls a face. "What you know about flavors marrying?"

My phone vibrates, and I look down quickly, my heart sinking when I see Orion's name on the screen instead of Grayson's. I haven't heard from her since last night when we spent the night on FaceTime, me, redlining briefs and returning client emails, her, sketching pieces for her next collection and listening to music. She'd hung up after about an hour or so, claiming to be run down from too many busy nights after the successful launch of Elysian weeks ago. I encouraged her to get some rest, telling her to sleep in for once in her life, which means I wasn't expecting to speak to her in the morning before work like usual, but now it's the early evening and I still haven't heard from her. I'm getting worried.

I pocket my phone and cross over into the living room, leaning over the back of the sectional. "Just something I heard on Food Network," I admit, making her bark out a laugh that quickly turns into a cough. I start to move towards her, but she holds out a hand to stop me.

"I'm fine, baby. I can't have you getting sick."

"Ma, I'll be fine. I came over here to take care of you, so let me do that, please."

Her frown is clear to me even through the mask covering her

mouth, and I can't help but laugh. She's so damn stubborn. Always convinced she's a burden, even when we all tell her we don't mind taking care of her.

"All I need is the flavors of your soup to finish their wedding, so you can fix me a bowl and get out of my hair."

"Damn, woman, it's like that?"

"Yes, it's like that. You got better things to do than sit around babysitting your mama."

"Not tonight, I don't."

She pushes up to her feet, shuffling over to the kitchen with the oversized knit blanket dragging on the floor behind her. "Yes, you do. You're just waiting for Grayson to let you know what that something better is."

"No, I'm not. Grayson is busy tonight, and I've already told her I've got my hands full with you."

I follow her into the kitchen, putting my hands on her shoulders to guide her to a seat at the island and away from the stove. She lands on the barstool with a huff but no argument and watches me round the counter to find a bowl for her soup. It's been on the stove for a while now, so it should be good to serve, but I still do another test taste before I fix her helping.

"When did you start getting bold enough to lie to your mama?" she asks, taking the bowl from my hands as soon as I bring it to her.

Instead of answering her question, I watch her take her first bite. "Is it good?"

"Doesn't taste like mine, but it'll do."

My amusement leaves me in a sharp huff as I move over to another cabinet and find a storage bowl large enough to hold the rest of the soup. Ma eats quietly as I put the leftovers away and go about washing up the last of the dishes and wiping down her counters. She's always been a stickler for cleaning, especially in the kitchen, so I take my time and disinfect every surface before moving on to sweeping the floor.

The tedium of cleaning is a nice distraction from Grayson's silence, but it only lasts for so long. As soon as I'm done washing Ma's bowl and spoon, I'm right back on my phone, checking to see if she's texted.

She hasn't.

"Just call the girl, Xavier," Ma says, on her feet again, but this time heading toward her bedroom. She doesn't even wait for me to respond, leaving me alone in the kitchen with only her suggestion and my phone for company. With a sigh, I unlock the screen and scroll until I find Grayson's name on my contact list. It wouldn't be the first time I've initiated a call between us, but somehow, in the face of her silence, it feels like it matters that I'm the one reaching out again.

I don't let myself think about it too much, don't listen to the voice in my head that tells me I'll look desperate if I call because I am a lot things for Grayson Hart, and desperate is definitely one of them.

The phone rings twice before she answers.

"Hel—" Her voice cracks around the end of the word. She sniffles and clears her throat, trying again. "Xavier, hey."

"What's the matter, baby?" I ask, bypassing all greetings and formalities.

Grayson sighs before responding, swallowing like it hurts to speak. "Flu."

I'm on my feet in an instant, the phone cradled between my shoulder and ear as I make my way to the fridge to pull out the soup I just put up. "You went to the doctor?"

"Mhm hmm," she hums. "They said it's going around."

"Yeah." I rush over to the cabinet where Ma keeps her Tupperware and take out a bowl big enough to hold a generous serving. "Ma has it too."

"Oh, no." I can hear the pout in her voice, and it makes me want to kiss her forehead. "Tell her I hope she feels better soon."

"Maybe you should worry about getting yourself better instead of sending someone else well wishes, Hart." The broth is still warm, and it splashes onto my skin as I scoop large spoonfuls of it into the bowl I've already made up in my mind is going to Grayson.

"I can do both, Allen. Is anyone with her? Somebody should be taking care of her."

The care and concern she has for my mother does something primal to me, and I wonder, not for the first time, how someone could be in possession of something as precious as her heart and abuse it so thoroughly.

"I came over and made her soup. She's resting now, but I'm going to get Chase or Lincoln to come and sit with her for the rest of the night."

"Why? Where are you going?"

It's such an innocent question, speaking so clearly of her unawareness of how deeply I care for her, and it gives me pause, forcing me to remember our agreement about taking things slow, keeping things "unserious" as Grayson would say. It's such a frustrating thing. To want so much with someone so afraid to let themselves have it, have you. But I'm committed to the cause, to taking my time with Grayson, to asking for permission to do things that my feelings for her spark a natural desire in me to perform.

"Well, I was hoping you'd let me come over and take care of you."

"Xavier, you don't have to—"

"But I want to, Hart. *I want to.*"

The line goes quiet. For a moment, I think she's going to refuse me, and I curse myself for coming on too strong, for being too upfront about my desire to take care of her when I know that she still has trouble accepting that kind of thing from a romantic partner. But then something miraculous happens. She pushes out a slow breath, considering the ramifications of accepting my offer. We would be in unfamiliar territory. She'd be welcoming me into her home without the pretense of sex to protect us from everything else we think of and feel for each other. I'd be dangerously close to showing the cards I've tried to play close to the vest.

We'd be making a mockery of every thing that has ever claimed to be un-serious.

"Okay," she says carefully. "Kendra and Chantel are here now, but they'll leave the door open for you."

"Sounds good. I'll be there as soon as I can." With my keys in one hand and the bowl of soup in the other, I make my way down the hall towards Ma's room. "Do you need anything else? Meds, tissues, Gatorade?"

"No." Her voice is soft with drowsiness, and I can tell she's fading, giving in to whatever medicine I'm sure her cousins plied her with. "Just you."

Although I'm certain an un-medicated Grayson would have never let those words slip past her lips, I can't help but smile when I hear them, a part of me comforted by the proof that she's as helpless as I am when it comes to this connection we have. When her soft snores fill the line, I end the call and knock on my mother's door, waiting for her permission before pushing it open to find her snuggled deep under the covers.

She takes one look at the smile on my face and laughs. "Let me guess, you took my advice and called Grayson and now you've got plans?"

"Not quite. She's sick, and I talked her into letting me come over to take care of her."

"Poor thing. She's been working too hard. Tell her she needs to make sure she's resting in between all those fancy fashion shows."

"I'll let her know, Ma."

"Alright. Well, I'll see you later, baby. Love you."

"Love you too." I blow her a kiss from the doorway, knowing she won't want me to come any closer now that she's taken her mask off. "I'll call to check on you in the morning, okay? Linc, Chase or O will be by later on tonight to see if you need anything."

I make the promise even though I haven't asked either of them if they're available to fulfill it because I know they will. After the years we spent without her, none of us take our mother's health, mental or physical, for granted. When she needs us, we always make a point to be there, even when she complains.

"Sounds good." She turns her back to me, closing her eyes. "Tell Grayson I said hello."

"Yes, ma'am."

* * *

As soon as I'm done locking up Ma's house, I send a text to the group chat to make sure someone will stop by and check in on her. Everyone replies at once, relaying their availability and by the time I get to Grayson's place, we have a care schedule lined up that will ensure Ma isn't alone for the next few days. I even manage to squeeze in a quick call to Lou, letting him know what's going on because I'm sure my stubborn mother didn't even bother to read her husband in.

My suspicions are confirmed when, as I'm walking up to Grayson's front door, I get a text from him thanking me for letting him know and promising to get an earlier flight back home. With all of my son duties done, I slide my phone into my back pocket and test the knob on Grayson's front door, finding it unlocked just like she promised it would be. The house is quiet when I step inside, and it smells like her. There are shoes under the bench by the front door, so I toe mine off and leave them with the others, padding over to the kitchen to reheat the soup and grab a spoon before heading up the stairs.

This is only my second time here, but the layout is simple, and it doesn't take me long to make my way to Grayson's bedroom. The door is cracked, and I can hear the TV playing in the background. I push the door open, expecting to find her sleeping, but instead, she's sitting up. Her back is against the headboard, and her arms are up while she tries to fix the messy bun on top of her head.

"You're supposed to be laying down," I say, moving over to her side of the bed. I place the bowl and spoon on her nightstand before planting a soft kiss on her overly warm forehead.

She swats me away. "Don't. You'll get sick."

I lean back in, brushing my lips over her temple. "Don't care."

"You should care. This flu is awful." Her hands are back in her hair the moment I pull back and take a seat on the edge of the bed. "I *feel* awful, and I'm sure I look even worse."

I'm certain there's no scenario in which she would look anything other than beautiful, but my eyes still sweep over her features to look for evidence to uphold her statement. Her hair is wild and frizzy, most of the perimeter refusing to be held by the satin hair tie she's used to make the bun. There's a bit of drool on the corner of her mouth and crusts of sleep in her left eye. Her skin isn't as vibrant as it usually is, and there's a glassiness to her eyes that always happens when someone is running a fever.

But even with all of that, she's still beautiful.

She's always beautiful.

"You're perfect."

Her arms drop to her sides, her hair forgotten. "You always say that."

"And I always mean it too." We're both quiet for a moment, staring at each other, contemplating what we are and what we'll be when this is all said and done. I know what I want, and I think, based on the way she's looking at me, Grayson knows, too. I also think she wants the same things, but now isn't the time for me to push her on that.

"When's the last time you ate?"

She bites her lips, casting her eyes up to the ceiling as she tries to recall. "Chantel force fed me a banana before she drove me to the doctor this morning."

I balk, reaching over to grab the bowl and spoon from her night-stand. "This morning?! It's almost seven, Hart."

"I know. I've been asleep for most of the day. That's why I missed all of your texts."

"I don't care about the texts, Grayson," I mutter, popping the top off the bowl and scooping up a spoonful of broth. "I care that you've been taking medicine on an empty stomach."

Her eyes narrow, telling me how much she resents being scolded, but she still opens up when I carefully bring the bite to her mouth. Her lips wrap around the spoon, and she moans with relief when she swallows, holding a hand to her throat.

"That feels nice. Thank you."

"You're welcome. Do you want more?" She nods, and I prepare another bite, spoon feeding her until her eyes are low with a renewed need for sleep. I rise to my feet, grabbing the lid for the bowl and reattaching it while Grayson watches me through rapidly fluttering lids. "Lay back down, baby."

She complies, sliding under the covers. "Will you hold me?"

God, my fucking heart can't take her like this. All soft and needy for me. It makes me want to say things I know I shouldn't say. I bite the inside of my cheek and hold up the bowl. "Of course, I will. Let me put this soup up first, okay?"

"Okay."

I take the stairs two at a time on the way down, making sure the house is secure before returning to Grayson's room to find her fighting sleep.

"Why are you still up, Hart?" I'm undoing my pants, refusing to get in her bed in my work clothes, and she smiles, hazy eyes following my every move as I strip down to nothing but a pair of briefs.

"I wanted to see the show."

"Pervert."

Grayson giggles as I slip between sheets that smell like her, wrapping one arm around her waist to pull her closer. We both let out a soft sigh when her head comes to rest on my chest. Sleep finds her almost instantly, but I lie awake for hours just to listen to her breathe, just to soak in the reality of being needed by a woman who's determined to never need a man again, trusted by a woman who's had her faith in another weaponized, and wanted by a woman I've craved since the day we met.

13

GRAYSON

old and flu medicine plus the persuasive rumble of Xavier's phone voice.

That's how I ended up here.

Here being, in my bed, my legs tangled up with his, my arms thrown over abs I don't even feel well enough to fully appreciate, with drool sliding down the side of my face onto his chest. I'm too tired, and far too sick, to be embarrassed, so I just lay there, breathing through my mouth because my nose is stopped up. It's dark. The only light in the room coming from the muted TV that's still playing Living Single re-runs.

"Your fever broke," Xavier says, touching a hand to my forehead.

I'm not surprised that he's awake. He strikes me as the type of person who would stay up all night just to avoid the narrow possibility of being asleep when the person under his care needs something.

"I'll have to take your word for it because I don't feel any different."

Well, that's not exactly true. Having him here makes me happier than I've been in days. Laying on his chest while he holds me close makes me feel precious, cared for, loved. As soon as the word pops up in my head, I push it back down and force myself up and out of the bed, putting some distance between Xavier and I.

He rises from his spot. His questioning gaze lit up by the flickering lights on the TV. "Where are you going?"

"Shower," I call out over my shoulder, rushing to the bathroom. I half expect him to follow me, but he doesn't. The door clicks closed behind me, and I lock it for good measure, not because I don't trust Xavier to respect my privacy, but because I don't trust myself not to go back out there and ask him if what's happening to me is also happening to him.

Not the fever induced sweats and the clogged nose that's turned me into a mouth breather, but the other stuff. The sweet, soft longing for his presence. The loud, insistent craving for his skin and his lips and his eyes and his voice. Every minute of my day is spent forcing myself not to think of him, not to text him back too quickly, not to smile too hard when I answer his daily FaceTime calls, not to invite him over for the sole purpose of breathing the same air as him.

I run a hand over my face and try to push a calming breath out through my nose, before remembering that both nostrils are congested and redirecting it to my mouth. I'm such a mess, and I never should have agreed to let Xavier come over to take care of me. Spending the night drooling on his chest is probably the least sexy, least un-serious thing I could ever do, and now the lines of our situation are blurred.

Haven't they always been blurred? I ask myself silently, shuffling over to the vanity to brush my teeth and wash my face. I feel a little more human once I've moisturized, able to acknowledge that Xavier was right about the fever breaking. My eyes are no longer glassy, and my limbs, while still heavy, don't ache as much as they did yesterday. I feel confident I can take a shower and maybe even wash my hair without passing out, so I go for it, moving as fast as my tired limbs will allow, trying to be quick and thorough.

When I finish, I wrap myself up in a towel, run a brush through my curls before putting it in another bun and heading back out into my bedroom to face Xavier. The sun is coming up now, bathing the room in gentle rays of light that spill over my bed, highlighting the fact that my mattress is now bare and my companion is nowhere to be found. I stand there, stunned, my sick brain trying to process all the changes, which is how Xavier finds me.

He comes striding into my room, still in those slutty little briefs he always wears, with a stack of fresh linens in hand and a serious look on his face. "You should sit down. You've probably been on your feet too long."

As if trying to prove his point, every muscle in my body starts to feel weak, so I sink down into the seat in front of my vanity, eyeing him suspiciously. "What'd you do to my sheets?"

He glances at me, brows folded with confusion, as he slides one corner of the fitted sheet onto the mattress. "Um, nothing?"

"Then why are you putting new ones on the bed?"

In all my years of marriage and cohabitation, I never once saw Brian strip or make a bed, so it strikes me as odd that Xavier would do it completely unprompted.

With the fitted sheet secured, Xavier reaches for the top sheet. "Because I figured you'd want fresh ones after your shower, and my mom always says you should change your sheets after your fever breaks, so you're not sleeping in old germs."

"Oh."

He straightens, tipping his head to one side as he tries to gauge my mood. "Oh?"

"Yeah. Oh." I grab the bottle of lotion on the vanity and pump some into my hands, refusing to meet his gaze as I slather it onto my skin.

"Are you weirded out by me changing your sheets, Hart?"

"What?! No, of course not. Why would that weird me out?"

"I don't know, but you've got a look on your face that tells me this —" he waves a hand over the bed, which is now covered in a fresh duvet "—is bringing up some feelings for you. I'm just not sure what they are."

The look he's talking about is in fact my 'in my feelings' face. However, none of the varying emotions running through me right now are anything close to weird or uncomfortable. If anything, I'm mad. At Brian, for never once showing up for me the way Xavier has in the short time I've known him and never so much as getting me a fucking tissue anytime I got sick. And at myself for wasting all those years on a selfish bastard when a man like this was out here waiting for me.

I can't say any of that to Xavier though, so once I'm done with my lotion and he's no longer busy putting new cases on the pillows, I just walk over and hug him. "Thank you for changing the bedding and for being here to take care of me. I appreciate you."

"You're welcome." He wraps his arms around me, placing a soft kiss on my forehead. "Does this mean you're not weirded out?"

"Quite the opposite. I'm very appreciative."

"So you won't find it odd if I run home, shower, grab my work stuff and come back to hang out with you for the rest of the day? Maybe even stay the whole weekend?"

"You don't—" I start, swallowing the rest of the sentence when he narrows his eyes at me. He hates when I tell him he doesn't have to do things he so clearly wants to do for me. I hate feeling odd about accepting his generosity, especially when he's always offering those parts of himself up to me so freely.

Is this what it's like? I wonder to myself. *Is this how it feels to be with a man who genuinely likes you?*

"I would love that," I say finally, earning myself a bright, warm smile from Xavier and a smacking kiss to my lips that makes me laugh before I scold him about putting himself at risk of getting sick. After we're both dressed, and I'm tucked back into bed with orders not to take any medicine until he returns with our breakfast, I burrow underneath the covers and start a group FaceTime with my cousins.

A'ja answers first, and the angle of her camera reveals that she's in her home office. Before we can even exchange greetings, Chantel comes on the line, her face on one side of the screen while Kendra's is on the other.

"What are y'all doing together and why wasn't I invited?" A'ja asks, her nose scrunched up.

"We told you we were going shopping for Crew's party decorations today," Kendra says, pointing an accusatory finger at A'ja through the screen. "*You* said you had to work."

"I do have to work. I also recall asking if y'all could wait until I wrapped up my day to go shopping, so I could be included. I mean, who buys party decorations at eight in the damn morning?"

Kendra turns the finger she was just using to antagonize A'ja into her own chest. "***ME!***"

Chantel grabs the phone, shifting Kendra out of the screen, so the situation doesn't escalate further. No one needs A'ja and Kendra on the outs, not with Crew's birthday in two weeks. He asked if he could have the party at my house, wanting to take advantage of the pool in my backyard, and because I can't deny him anything—even a request for a bouncy house Kendra gave me hell about—I said yes.

"A'ja, don't be mad at Ken. I'm the one that asked her to meet me because it's the only time I'd be available this week."

Unimpressed by Chantel's plea, A'ja purses her lips and arches a brow, refusing to say a word. Since I started the call, I feel obligated to try to calm things down, or at least change the subject to make them forget what they're fighting about.

"Xavier's spending the weekend over here," I blurt out, covering my face with the covers.

"He knows you're sick, right? Like he's not expecting no coochie or nothing?"

"A'ja!" Chantel gasps, fighting back a laugh.

"What? I'm just asking a question. I don't want him thinking she's going to be busting it wide open all weekend when she can't even breathe properly."

Kendra shoves her way back onto the screen just so we can see her rolling her eyes. "He knows she's sick, A'ja. He came over yesterday to take care of her. By the way, how'd that go?"

"It was great. He fed me homemade chicken noodle soup and held me all night." The words come out in a love sick gush that sounds even more disgusting thanks to my stuffy nose, but I can't stop myself from continuing. "And this morning, he changed the sheets on the bed while I was in the shower. Isn't that sweet?"

"Oh, *honey*," A'ja murmurs, her voice laced with the mix of pity and excitement I see in all of their eyes. As sad as it sounds, I've gotten used to these expressions. When they appear, it's to remind me of all the common place, mundane experiences Brian robbed me of, and to let me know how happy the people who love me are about me getting to have them now.

"That is sweet, Gray," Chantel says, stretching her eyes wide to get A'ja in line.

"Very sweet," A'ja agrees quickly.

"When are you two going to admit that you're in love?" Kendra asks, shocking no one. Ever since I've started teasing her about her "friendship" with Orion, she's taken to pressing me about my feelings for Xavier.

"We're not in love."

As usual, my denial is met with my cousins' skepticism, and because I don't have the energy to go back and forth with them, I remain quiet.

"Maybe not yet, but you're definitely on your way," Chantel argues. I open my mouth to respond, but think better of continuing the conversation when I hear the front door open and close.

"I have to go. I think Xavier's back."

We all say quick goodbyes and hang up just as Xavier comes into the room. He's wearing gray sweats, a matching hoodie and a pair of white Nikes that look like he just pulled them out of the box. There's a book bag on his back, a duffel slung over his shoulder, and what looks like a grocery bag in his hand. I sit up a little, leaning against the headboard as I watch him set his things down next to the side of the bed he's claimed as his own.

"That was a quick trip."

"I didn't want to keep you waiting."

He sets the grocery bag on the bed and begins to unpack it, pulling out a container of fresh cut fruit, a smaller bag with wrapped breakfast sandwiches, that smell faintly of bacon, and a few pastries. My stomach rumbles, and Xavier laughs.

"I guess I was right to rush." He hands me one sandwich and slides the fruit and pastries closer to me as I unwrap it. "Eat. I'm going to run downstairs and get your medicine and something to drink. Do you want anything specific? Coffee, juice, water? I could make you some tea."

My mouth is full of buttery biscuit, savory bacon and cheesy eggs, so I can't exactly formulate a response. Xavier doesn't seem to mind, and he doesn't wait for me to finish chewing before he leaves the room, chuckling. Moments later, he comes back with a tray of assorted drinks—some of which were not in my refrigerator the last time I checked—napkins, utensils for us to eat the fruit with, and my medicine. I gape at him, and he gives me a sheepish grin as he hands me the pills.

"I may have a gotten a little carried away with the drinks, but I wanted you to have options."

"Options are good," I muse, taking a glass of orange juice. The first sip of the acidic drink coupled with the scrape of the assortment of pills burns a bit when I swallow, and I wince.

"You good? Want something different?"

"No, I'll be fine."

"Are you sure because—"

"Xavier, sit down, eat, and stop fussing over me."

He holds his hands up in mock surrender, a smile on his lips as he rounds the bed and takes his place beside me. "Somebody's feeling better. I guess the Allen Rehabilitation Program is working."

A stupid smile tugs on my lips, and I don't even bother trying to hide it. "Shut up."

"Yeah." He takes a bite of his sandwich, a proud and annoying grin warming the side of my face. "It's definitely working."

14

XAVIER

ndrew Savage, the founding partner of my firm and my mentor, once told me that a man in love is a man at risk of losing his sanity. It was a random statement meant to teach me some abstract lesson about a client's state of mind that I put out of my head immediately because I realized early in life that most people view love as a weapon and yield it as one.

That's what my father had done. Fashioned his love into a blade that cut my mother down to the quick, stealing her confidence and joy, making it so she didn't trust herself to take care of us even though he didn't want to. Somewhere along the way, between my fucked up childhood and the height of my career, I decided that love wasn't for me, which meant I would never be at risk of losing my sanity.

That was true until I met Grayson, and now I'm certain I've lost my mind because I've allowed her to talk me into attending a seven-year-old's birthday party. Actually, attend is the wrong word because between Orion and I, we're caught somewhere between hosts and entertainment, keeping the group of thirty or so kids busy while Grayson, Kendra, and every other adult besides us, hides from the heat inside the house.

Sweat beads on the back of my neck, and I just let it because there's no point in fighting back against August heat. You never win. Even when you're in the pool wearing nothing but a pair of swimming trunks.

"Alright, alright, last round of Marco Polo," O yells, clapping his hands to get the attention of the group of kids floating or standing in the water between us.

I'm at the back, where the water is deepest, and Orion is standing in the shallow end, his hands on the shoulders of Kendra's son, Crew. I've always known O was good with kids—he has a ton of nieces and nephews that adore him— but I've never seen him like he is with Crew. It feels almost paternal. Now that I know about whatever is going on with him and Kendra, I hear about Crew all the time—*Made a Roblox account, so I could play with Crew. Can't meet tonight, I promised Crew we'd FaceTime and watch anime before bed. Think I might sign up to coach rec basketball again because Crew wants to play*—but this is my first time seeing them interact, and it's obvious to me they've developed a strong bond.

I just hope it'll be able to stay intact if things don't work out between him and Kendra.

O leans down, looking the birthday boy in the eye. "Ready, kid?"

Crew nods quickly but doesn't begin counting down immediately. Instead, he catches my eye. "Can we do it in Japanese again?"

"Of course. How about you start, and I'll jump in if you get mixed up?"

His answering grin is wide, filled with gaps from where he's lost his two front teeth, and I smile back, proud to have found a point of connection with a kid that means so much to two of the most important people in my life. I don't even know how I ended up revealing that I speak Japanese, but Crew latched on to the fact, supplying me with word after word to translate for him and his friends as they ran between the bouncy house and pool.

"Close your eyes first," O reminds him. "Everyone, get ready to scatter."

A slew of excited giggles sounds out around us, but I stay focused on Crew. His eyes are closed now, and his voice is tentative when he begins to count.

"Ichi." *One.* "Ni." *Two.* "San." *Three.* "Shi." *Four.* "Go." *Five.* "Roku." *Six.* "Shichi." *Seven.* He pauses, brows folding into a hard line as he tries to recall what comes next.

"Hachi," I say, supplying the word for eight.

"Hachi," Crew repeats, his body swaying a little in the water. Orion says he does that when he gets nervous. "Kyuu." *Nine.* I find myself mouthing the final words with him, giving him a nod of encouragement even though he can't see me. "Juu!" he shouts triumphantly, stopping the count at ten before launching himself into the water and hunting down his friends with a ruthlessness Orion is still bragging to Kendra about as he carries Crew to her car when they leave for the night.

When they're gone, I lock up and join Grayson in the living room where she's relaxing with a much deserved glass of wine. Even though it wasn't her kid's party, she put in a lot of work to make the day special for Crew and stress-less for Kendra. I can see that it's all catching up with her now. I take a spot on the couch too, pulling her feet into my lap to massage them.

She closes her eyes and sighs. "That feels nice."

"Do you want me to run you a bath so you can really relax?"

"I would love that," she says, peeking at me through heavy lids. "But I have to wash up the few dishes Mom couldn't fit in the dishwasher."

After the party was done, Grayson's mom, aunts, and cousins worked with us to return the house to its usual pristine condition. They would have stuck around to do the last few things, but Grayson wouldn't let them, insisting she was going to leave everything else until tomorrow. I knew she was lying then, which is why I planned to take care of it tonight.

"I'm going to do that. *You're* going to take a bath and get in bed, and when I'm done, I'm going to come up and eat your pussy because we both know you sleep better after you've had an orgasm."

The way she reacts when I talk so openly about eating her out will never get old to me. No matter what she's doing or where we are, it's always the same thing. The slow trickle of heat that turns her eyes into twin pools of desire. The slight parting of her lips and the subtle shift in her breathing that makes her breasts rise and fall just a bit quicker. Everything about it is real and raw and *mine*.

Grayson reaches down and grabs the hem of her sundress—which to no one's surprise is black and perfectly tailored to her curves—hiking it up and exposing her thick thighs and the tiny scrap of fabric covering her mound. She lets her legs fall apart, forcing me to notice the way the poor excuse for a pair of underwear leaves her pussy lips partially on display.

"Or you could eat my pussy now."

I'm between her legs in an instant, shifting her underwear to the side and pulling her clit into my mouth. Grayson arches up off the couch, her shocked gasp hitting the ceiling before raining down around us.

"Fuck. Xavier. Wait, I—" She squirms underneath my ministrations, trying to get away from the unrelenting strokes of my tongue across the sensitive bundle of nerves. I pull back a bit, just long enough to watch her face when I say, "This is what you wanted, Hart. Don't run from me when I'm giving you what you asked for."

Then I'm back on her, licking, sucking, nipping until there's a puddle of her essence on the couch underneath her ass and her legs are shaking around my ears. And even then, I don't stop. I kiss the inside of her thighs and drive into her soft, silken heat with two fingers while she grips her breasts and rolls her hips, trying to match my movements to maximize her pleasure.

"You're incredible, Grayson. Tell me you know that."

She gives me a jerky nod, eyes still squeezed tight as I stroke in and out of her. "I know," she gasps, a rough moan falling from her lips when my fingers start to focus on that ridged flesh at the front of her walls.

"Say it," I demand, bringing my mouth back to her clit as her sex begins to tremble around my fingers.

"*Xavier,*" she pleads, frustration laced with pleasure leaving her body in a huff. She hates when I do this, when I make her speak love and positivity into herself, when all she wants to do is come. As far as timing goes, I know there are better moments to have her repeat affirmations, but there's something so fucking sexy to me about hearing Grayson's proclamations of self-love blend with the frayed edges of an orgasm.

"Say. It." I curl my fingers inside of her, emphasizing the verbal request, and she bucks against me wildly, grinding her sex into my face and onto my fingers, trying to chase down her release without my assistance, which only makes me want to withhold it.

My hand goes still, and my mouth hovers just a few inches away from where she needs me. Grayson sits up, eyes wild and disbelieving. "*Xavier, please.*"

"You know what I want to hear, Hart."

She throws herself back against the cushions. "I'm incredible," she huffs, rolling her eyes and then moaning when I start to work her over once again.

"Say it like you mean it, baby," I coach her.

"I'm incredible," she repeats, this time with more feeling.

"Again."

"I'm incredible."

"Again, Grayson. Say I'm incredible."

"*I'm incredible,*" she says, the declaration breaking over a moan.

I reward her obedience by finger fucking her faster, sucking her clit harder, keeping the pace and pressure consistent while she sobs through one orgasm and then another. When it's all said and done, Grayson is boneless and sated, which means she doesn't argue or protest when I usher her upstairs and run her a bubble bath.

"Join me," she says from inside the large, freestanding tub where there's more than enough room for the both of us.

"I would love to, Hart, but I've got dishes to wash."

Lifting one bubble covered hand out of the water, she reaches for me with a seductive pout on her lips. "The dishes can wait."

"Fine, I'll join you." She does a little celebratory shimmy, and I laugh as I strip down. "You have to promise that you won't try to sneak downstairs in the morning and wash those dishes, though."

Grayson places her hand over her heart, watching me sink into the water. "I promise."

I squint at her, suspicious by how quickly she's folded. "Why don't I believe you, Hart?"

"I don't know, Allen." She nudges me with her foot, and I catch it underneath the water, tickling the sole just to make her giggle. "Why didn't I know you speak Japanese?"

My multilingual status was revealed to her by Crew as he shoved birthday cake into his mouth. She'd lifted her brows at me but said nothing. I knew it was going to come up again, though.

"I don't know. I wasn't intentionally keeping it from you. I guess it just never came up."

Silence stretches between us as we both consider all the things that haven't come up in conversation in the time we've known each other. Given the way we met, I think there are probably more blanks on my side than on Grayson's, which makes me feel like I have an unfair advantage. She must feel the same way too, because her eyes are now sparkling with curiosity.

"Do you speak any other languages?"

"Spanish. A little German. Some Mandarin."

"Did you learn because you wanted to or because of your job?" she asks, pushing up out of the water and gliding through it to get to me. I watch, mesmerized, as bubbles and droplets of moisture slide off of her breasts and onto my chest as she straddles me. My hands go to her hips, and I gaze up at her, conscious of the fact that the tip of my dick is grazing her pussy.

"A little of both," I grit out, losing my train of thought when she reaches down and grips my length, positioning me underneath her. "What are you doing, Hart?"

Her teeth are digging into her bottom lip, a telltale sign of deviance, but she still bats her lashes at me innocently. "Listening to you, of course."

"I don't think that's true." The words come out rough and my fingers flex against her skin as she hovers above me, teasing me with the possibility of feeling her with nothing between us. We've talked around this topic. The whole no condom thing. I've proven that I'm clean, and Grayson has as well, but somehow we've never actually leaned into what that could mean, how that could change sex for us.

I've been content to leave the decision with her, and now, at the moment when I least expected, she's decided.

Her nails score the skin on my shoulders as she sinks down onto me. The first few inches are always the hardest for her, so she goes slow, allowing herself time to adjust. I have to force myself to relinquish my hold on her, to give her space to move, and the rhythm she sets is punishing. Every rock of her hips is powerful, sending water sloshing over the sides of the tub, taking my self control with it.

"Fuck, Hart," I groan, already feeling that bolt of lightning down my spine. "You feel too good."

"Say something."

Any other moment, any other encounter, and I would have been able to make sense of her words, but this moment is unlike any other. There's so much to hear and feel. The steady slap of water landing on the tile. Grayson's warm, slick body moving against mine. Her pussy gripping my dick like a vise.

"What?"

"In Japanese or any of the other languages. Say something. Anything," she says, her breath catching in her lungs when I start to fuck up into her. "I just want to…fuck, Xavier, please."

There's nothing left. My self control is shattered, lying in pieces on the wet tile of Grayson's bathroom, so when she starts to beg, I don't think, I just act. I just give in to that part of me that's committed to giving Grayson everything she wants, no matter what it costs me.

Helpless, I groan the first words that come to mind into her ear.

"Aishiteru wa."

I love you.

15

GRAYSON

I love you.

Two days after our little bathtub escapade, I looked up the words Xavier uttered into my ear that night. With only his pronunciation to go off of, it took me forever to spell it out, but eventually I got it. We were on the phone when it happened, FaceTiming because he's been out of town for work and I missed having his eyes on me, and I almost died from shock.

Immediately, I started to question whether or not he meant it, or if I had heard him correctly, but when I asked him just to be sure, he repeated it, his inflection a perfect replica of the tone the man used in the pronunciation video I played out loud after I got him off the phone. Nearly a week has gone by since then, and neither of us have mentioned it, but this morning, just before he boarded his flight back home, Xavier texted me to ask if I knew what it meant yet.

I didn't respond.

I couldn't.

Because I couldn't shake the feeling that this wasn't how things with him were supposed to go. I laid down the ground rules, said all the words to subtract meaning and circumvent emotion, did all the things I was supposed to do to keep him at arm's length, but somehow he still stole his way into my heart. And now he's commandeered my thoughts, making it impossible for me to focus on work even though I promised my manufacturer I'd have new designs to them by the end of the day, so they can get started on the new samples.

Somewhere along the way, I got it in my head that I could make the samples myself, that the act of cutting, pinning and sewing would ease my troubled mind. I was wrong. Well, not completely. The moment I walked into the fabric store, I felt the familiar sense of peace wash over me. The trouble is, that peace went floating away on a cloud of confusion when Brian and Noelle walked onto the same aisle as me. I saw them before they saw me, noting that the sight of their linked hands no longer stings the way it used to, and decided to speak because I refused to do something weird like run away.

Pulling a bolt of maroon satin off of the shelf so I can have it cut later, I aim a calm smile in their direction. "Brian. Noelle. Hey."

Both of their heads turn at the same time, Brian's gray-green gaze wide with genuine surprise while Noelle's brown eyes narrow. She lets him drop her hand and come to me, and I take stock of the way my body feels as he approaches. There's nothing there. No wave of self-consciousness. No fear of being found imperfect and wanting. No love. No hate.

No, nothing.

It's startling, being so unaffected by him after years of having my every thought, every feeling, every mood controlled by the look on his face. *Damn,* I think to myself, *I guess this is what it feels like to be healed.* The thought brings a smile to my face, and judging by the way Brian's eyes light up when he sees it, he thinks that smile is for him.

"Grayson." He comes in for a hug, but I step out of his reach. I might not hate the man anymore, but that doesn't mean I want his hands on me. "Sorry," he says, shrugging. "Old habits die hard, I guess."

"So I've been told."

There's no point in mentioning that I have firsthand experience that's taught me how true the old adage is. That he was an old habit I had to break and some days I thought the fight to disentangle myself from the woman who wanted to stay attached to him more than anything would kill me.

He shoves his hands into his pockets, running an assessing gaze over my frame. "You look good."

My outfit is nothing special, just a pair of leggings and an oversized hoodie, so I assume he's referring to the glow everyone says I have around me these days. The bright aura that comes from finally getting what you deserve out of life.

"Thanks. I guess that's what therapy and having your pussy eaten on the regular will do for you."

Noelle coughs loudly, and when I glance in her direction, her eyes are bugged out like she's choking on air. She recovers quickly, and I swear I see jealousy flash in her eyes before she turns her back to me.

Brian gawks at me, his eyes as wide as his girlfriend's. "You're dating?"

"Yes, Brian. I'm dating."

Though that feels like too light a word for what Xavier and I are doing. If I'm being honest with myself, I know that it always was. We were never just dating. Never just fucking. Never just un-serious. We were courting a future, flirting with the idea of forever. We were falling in love.

"Who?" The question hits me with the force of a demand we both know he has no right to make anymore. My brows raise, silently imploring him to reconsider his tone and maybe the question altogether. A muscle in his jaw pulses, but again, his annoyance has no power over me. "If you don't mind sharing," he adds, more desperate for information than he is to keep his pride intact.

"No, I don't mind sharing at all. It's actually someone you know."

"You're dating one of my friends? Grayson, that's just—"

"You and Xavier have never been friends," I say, cutting him off before he can get too deep into his tirade because he should know that I wouldn't touch the men he considers friends with a ten-foot pole.

Brian rears back as if I've slapped him. "Xavier Allen? Your divorce lawyer?"

"One in the same."

Another pulsing of his muscle, another clench of his jaw before he says, "Well, *that's* a choice."

I've been aware of Brian's hatred for Xavier for a long time now, but getting to see it eat him alive, getting to watch his face fall as he realizes he has, once again, lost to a man who doesn't consider him worthy enough to be his rival, will never get old. A sick kind of gratification runs through me as I realize that man is mine, and the sorry excuse for a human in front of me is not.

The ties have been cut.

The bonds have been broken.

And now, I'm free. Free to live and to love, free to speak my desires and trust that they'll be met, free from the cloud of shame and insecurity I've lived under since I made the grave error of loving Brian Lucas, but most of all, free to say what I really think about the sham of a union in front of me.

"So is going back to a woman who cheated on you with your roommate and came crawling back over a decade later with her hand out," I toss back, pairing the jab with a nasty, cutting smile that's the last thing he sees before I maneuver around him and walk away, leaving him alone with Noelle and the rest of his questionable choices.

After the fabric store, I head home, intending to shower and change into something a little sexier before going over to Xavier's and telling him I love him too. But when I pull up to the house, his car is already in the driveway. As soon as I put the car in park, he's at my door, pulling it open. It's been a long travel day for him, but he still looks immaculate, like he could have stepped off of the plane and gone straight into the courtroom, but instead he came to me. My heart squeezes when our eyes lock, and I can't fight the stupid grin curving my lips.

Xavier reaches for me, his hand coming up to grip my jaw as he runs a thumb over my lips. "Happy to see me, Hart?"

I turn, pressing a kiss into his palm. "Always."

"You never returned my text."

"I know. I had to do some thinking before I sent a response."

His eyes search my face, trying to decipher my mood. "And did you?"

"Send a response? No."

A soft chuckle passes through his lips. "I know you didn't send a response, Hart. I'm asking if you did all the thinking you needed to do."

Maybe it's his eyes or his voice or the love lining his features as he looks at me or the fact that I haven't been this close to him in almost a week, but I'm melting under the weight of his presence. And my heart is racing, smacking against my ribs as I fight for focus and some semblance of cool.

"Yeah, I think so."

Xavier breathes out a slow, steadying breath. "So you can confirm for me that you know the English translation for *aishiteru wa*?"

"I do."

"Tell me."

"It means I love you."

He runs his tongue across his bottom lip. "And I said that to you."

"You did."

"Because I do."

"Love me?"

He nods. "Yes, Hart. I love you."

God, his face. His expression is so open, so vulnerable, so scared. Like he thinks I might reject him, that I might hurt him, that I might not be able to trust him with my heart. I'm eager to tell him I already have.

"I love you too," I say softly. Simply. Because that's what he taught me love could be. The words are light on my tongue, costing me nothing but giving me everything, including the power not just to speak love, but to believe that I deserve it.

16

XAVIER

Two Years Later: Valentine's Day

"There's no one here," Grayson whispers to me as we climb the steps of the theater to claim spots on our favorite row. Like our first time at The Reel together, she's carrying the drinks, and I have the popcorn and the pleasure of watching her ass bounce in the leggings she always wears to our mid-week, early afternoon movie dates.

"Well, it is a weekday, Hart."

"I know, but it's Valentine's Day," she glances at me from over her shoulder, eyes stretched for emphasis. "Even if it is a weekday, you can't tell me it's not odd that no one is here."

Personally, I don't find it odd at all, mainly because I paid a handsome fee for us to have the theater to ourselves to celebrate the day and place where we had what I consider our first date. The date on the calendar had escaped my notice on that day two years ago, but I can't lie and say I would have done anything differently if I had known that I was spending private, personal time with a client on a day globally recognized for its romantic themes.

As a matter of fact, I know I wouldn't have. Grayson and I would have still shared laughs and popcorn and the meal I didn't eat. And we still would have wound up here, happy, in love, and hopefully, once it's all said and done, engaged. A nervous thrill runs through me, causing my stomach to clench as we settle into our seats and the lights begin to go down.

"Damn, that was fast," Grayson says, digging into her popcorn and doing a little happy dance as the first hit of the cinnamon and sugar combination she's addicted to hits her tongue. "They really said sit your ass down and watch this movie."

I try to laugh at her silly statement. Really, I do. But I can't because my heart is beating so damn fast and loud it's all I can do to stay in my seat and keep the question I've wanted to ask her for so long locked between my lips.

"You okay, babe?" Concern etches itself into Grayson's features as she conducts a visual examination. "You're not still feeling sick, are you? I told you we didn't have to come to the movies today. I was fine with waiting until this weekend to do something."

The sick she's referring to is the anxiety that's had me fighting mild panic attacks I've had to pass off as a stomach bug or virus of some kind. For days now, she's been hyper aware of every shift in my mood or expressions, which would be nice any other time, but it's hard to talk yourself through nerves about proposing to your girlfriend when she's always around, force feeding you ginger ale and chicken noodle soup your mother made even though she, and everyone else in your respective families, knows you're not sick, you're just scared shitless.

"No, I'm fine, baby." In order to sell the story, I reach for her left hand and bring her knuckles to my mouth, laying kisses on her skin. "Let's just enjoy the movie."

Unbeknownst to Grayson, the movie in question is a short film that I made with Amina's help. All the actors are people we know personally. All the lines are words I've already said to her face at some point in the time we've known each other.

When I pitched the idea to everyone, promising it would take minimal time and effort from them, they all agreed eagerly. Of course, both of our mothers tried to talk me into doing something a little more public, hoping they'd be able to play a bigger role in the day. I shut that down immediately, though, because I have firsthand knowledge of just how many public proposals end in bitter divorces.

Plus, I wanted to be sure that Grayson didn't feel pressured to give me her yes. She's been so much better about speaking up for herself, advocating for what she wants and needs from me, but I would never want to spend my life wondering if the presence of our loved ones influenced her choice to become my wife.

My high quality, but still homemade, film begins to play, and Grayson gasps when she sees her mother's face on the screen. Lottie is sitting beside Ma, both of them giddy as they clutch the paper with their lines on it.

"What in the world?" Grayson murmurs under her breath, loud enough for me to hear, but low enough not to compromise the audio booming around us.

"Grayson," our mother's say in unison. "Xavier wants you to know you're the most beautiful woman he's ever seen."

"Xavier, what is this?" she asks, eyes still on the screen where her aunts and cousins are.

"Grayson," Kendra, Chantel and A'ja say together. Their voices a quiet boom filled with love. "Xavier wants you to know you're the strongest woman he's ever known," Aunt Nita and Marcel add, before disappearing from the screen.

There are tears shining in her eyes, and she's so enthralled with the people on the screen and the things they're saying, she doesn't notice when I drop her left hand and slide out of my seat, dropping down to one knee on the ground in front of her while Orion, Lincoln, Chase and Crew tell her I love her more than I've ever loved anyone.

I pull the ring box out of the pocket of my sweats, popping it open just as my own disembodied voice fills the room.

"Grayson," I say on the video. "I have one question for you—"

The video stops there, and her head swings over in my direction. When she finds me down on one knee, a sob falls from her lips.

"Oh, my God."

"Will you marry me?" I ask, hand shaking, voice cracking like I've never asked a life-changing question before. "I know you've done the marriage thing before, and I get why you wouldn't want to do it again, but I just wanted to know if maybe you had it in you to try again, to try with me? I promise I will love you and protect you and uplift you. I promise that I'll support your dreams and champion your work. I'll give you babies if you want them or a cute dog or two if you don't. I'll rub your feet and run your baths and wash all the dishes that won't fit in the dishwasher. *I'll take care of you, Hart,* for the rest of our lives. And I promise I'll do that even if you don't take this ring from me today because the legality is all just icing on top of a cake I gorge myself on every day." I stop, taking a moment to gather myself, to breathe. "You can say no, and nothing between us will change, but I wouldn't be able to live with myself if I didn't ask if you want me to be your husband, if, maybe, you want to be my wife?"

Grayson slides to the edge of her seat, her fingers shaking as they grab hold of both sides of my face. She bites her lip, tears rolling down both cheeks. "As far as closing arguments go, this is probably your sloppiest work," she teases, pulling a nervous laugh out of me. "But," she continues, "you get bonus points for an emotional delivery and the beautiful ring."

"Hart," I plead because I can't go another second without knowing her answer, and I'm pretty sure there's a popcorn kernel under my knee. *"Please, answer the question."*

"Yes," she says quickly. "Yes, Xavier, I want you to be my husband. Yes, I want to be your wife. More than I've ever wanted anything."

THE END

ALSO BY J.L. SEEGARS

ABOUT THE AUTHOR

J.L. Seegars is a dedicated smut peddler and lifelong nerd who's always had a love of words, storytelling and drama. When she isn't writing messy and emotionally complex characters like the ones she grew up around, she's watching reality TV, supporting her fellow authors by devouring their work or spending time with her husband and son.